Midnight Stories

SU TONG

Translated by
Honey Watson

SINOIST

Published by Sinoist Books (an imprint of ACA Publishing Ltd)
London - Beijing
info@alaincharlesasia.com ☎ +44 20 3289 3885
www.sinoistbooks.com

Published by Sinoist Books (an imprint of ACA Publishing Ltd) in
arrangement with People's Literature Publishing House

Author: Su Tong **Translator:** Honey Watson **Editor:** Martin Savery

Original Chinese Text © 夜间故事 *(yejian gushi)* 2018, People's Literature
Publishing House, China

English Translation text © 2024 ACA Publishing Ltd, London, UK. A catalogue
record for *Midnight Stories* is available from the National Bibliographic Service
of the British Library.
This novel is entirely a work of fiction. The names, characters and incidents
portrayed in it are the work of the author's imagination. Any resemblance to
actual persons, living or dead, events or localities is entirely coincidental.

Paperback ISBN: 978-1-83890-541-5
eBook ISBN: 978-1-83890-542-2
Hardback ISBN: 978-1-83890-596-5

Supported using public funding by
ARTS COUNCIL
ENGLAND

*Sinoist Books is honoured to be supported using public
funding by Arts Council England.*

Midnight Stories

Su Tong

TRANSLATED BY
Honey Watson

SINOIST BOOKS

I

Tell Them I Was
Carried Away By
The White Crane

告诉他们
我乘白鹤去了

His sons and daughters have never seen the white crane, they have lived for quite some years, but in none of them have they ever seen the white crane. The old man says that every day at dusk the white crane comes to the pond to drink, it stands three steps away from that walnut tree with its soft feathers whiter and purer than newly rolled cotton. It submerges its beak. Sometimes a frog will emerge from that waterlogged grass along the bank and it will spread its wings and fly away, other times the oxen will low and it will spread its wings and fly away. The old man has been describing this scene of the white crane to his family since spring, but they have never seen it for themselves.

The old man stood three steps away from that walnut tree with his hands clasped behind his back. He was looking for a trace of the white crane's visit, a footprint or a feather in its wake, some evidence that it had come at all; such a pity that the crane was in such a hurry that it had left him nothing. But the old man could not doubt his own eyesight, his entire life he had relied upon his eyes to watch the weather, watch his crops, watch people come and go, and at seventy-three years of age, his eyes were as bright and clear as ever. Whoever said that his vision was dimming with old age, well, they themselves must be going blind.

That same old man paced a few times around the base of the walnut tree, his head turned toward it, no trace of those white feathers in the branches or their leaves either. He looked until his neck was sore and reached up to massage it, slowly leaning to sit against the trunk. It was dusk again, and the clouds piled upon the horizon like firewood waiting to be burned. This country, these trees, that pond and those houses with which he was all so familiar, let out a deep sigh, a sound which only he could hear. His children had ears but they did not hear it, they could not believe that their home sighed in the darkening light. The old man was still leaning against the walnut tree trunk. He took out a long-stemmed pipe and inhaled a few puffs which brought coughs rolling violently out of his throat. He felt that their strength shook even the tree behind him. Maybe his daughter was right about smoking when she said that his body was half ruined with smoke and that he shouldn't do it any more. The old man took the tobacco from the pipe's bowl and threw it to the ground, then quickly picked it up again thinking, what was that all about? Have I really gone senile, how could I throw away perfectly good tobacco?

An expression of self-reproach congealed on his old face as he sat there beneath the walnut tree. The people who till the fields facing the pond had already gone home, his children had gone, too. Apart from this churned black earth and the deep sighs which emerge from the dark recesses of this tilled ground, all was silent, even the sun was sinking quietly over the end of the earth. He wanted to wait out there until the sky was black, but his children would come and call him in for dinner. They meant him no harm and did not think that he was sick but they said to him:

"Grandpa, come home and eat, come and rest."

They had no idea what he was thinking. Who could? The walnut tree knows, the white crane who stands beneath it knows, but they cannot speak, and if they could speak then his children would still not understand, they cannot hear, they cannot believe that the white crane comes. The old man listened to his family's voices as they called to him. He stood and, before leaving the tree, picked up a walnut branch.

Finally, he walked a few steps between the tree and the pond. He used the branch to draw a large circle in the earth where he stood.

Now, a little boy catches loach by the side of the pond, a little girl catches butterflies beneath the walnut tree, these are that old man's grandchildren, he has brought them to see the white crane, of which they have not yet seen a trace; he leans against the tree and sleeps.

"Why won't the white crane come?" The little girl has not caught the butterfly she was after, so she reaches instead for the old man's ear. "You said that the white crane would be here, why can't I see it?"

"The sun's still burning bright, the white crane will not come." The old man cracks his eyelids and gazes towards the sky, saying: "It will come back from the mountains when the sun sets."

"Where does the white crane live? In the mountains?" asks the little girl.

"No, the white crane flew from very far away, and must fly all the way back there, too," says the old man. "Even I don't know where the white crane lives, it could be a thousand miles away, a place we can't even see.

The little boy catches a loach, he bundles it into his clothing and comes to show it to the old man as if it were the spoils of war.

"I caught a loach," he says to his grandpa. "If you chop it up and throw it in the water, the big bird will come back, big birds like eating loach better than anything else."

"It's not a big bird," says the old man. "It's a white crane, a white crane is the most blessed bird of all, from wherever the white crane flies, a person will be carried to heaven."

"Do you want the white crane to carry you to heaven?" asks the little boy.

"Yes, but I don't know if it will come for me." A sad smile drifts across the old man's lips. "It's not just anyone who can ride the white crane, I daren't even hope that I could." He stands and walks a few steps around the edges of the white circle. "But I won't let them drag me to Xiguan."

"What are they dragging you to Xiguan for?" asks the little boy. "Who wants to drag you to Xiguan?"

"Xiguan has a crematorium." The old man gestures and issues the crackling sound of flame from his mouth, saying: "People who go to Xiguan get turned into black smoke. Your father, your uncle, your aunt, they're all waiting for me to die to drag me to Xiguan. They've decided they're going to give me to the crematorium."

"If you don't want to go then don't go," the little boy chuckles as he realises his own mistake. "If you're dead, you can't move," the little boy says. "I understand, if you're dead, you have to go wherever they want you to."

"Yes, I'll go wherever it is they want me to go." The old man ruffles his grandson's hair as another bout of violent coughing erupts from his chest and, spluttering with every word, the old man holds his throat as he rasps: "I'll let them... the grown... ups... they... want... turn me into... smoke...

The little boy discovers that his grandpa's eyes are filled with tears and uses his hand to wipe them away. "Don't be scared," says the little boy, trying to soothe his grandpa. "They're just scaring you, how can people get turned into smoke? People can't turn to smoke."

"People can turn into smoke." The old man's coughing

has finally stopped and he leans against the tree. "People can turn into smoke."

Dragonflies flit across the surface of the pond, lying between banks where that year's millet has already begun to sprout, dandelions push their yellow heads into the sky where the spring's evening sun illuminates these three figures, all that young life growing around a seventy-three-year-old man. He raises his hand to wave, then leans on the walnut tree and closes his eyes, the little girl's voice wakes him as soon as he falls asleep.

She jumps in and out of the circle, raising her voice to say: "Why have you drawn a big circle here?"

"Don't play in the middle of it." The old man opens his eyes, shaking his head at the little girl, saying: "That is your grandpa's place, don't play inside it."

"Is this where you sleep?" the little girl asks. "We have a bed in the house, the bed is where you sleep, isn't it?"

"Wait until your grandpa is dead, and then he won't sleep in the house." The old man shakes his head as he speaks. "Your grandpa will sleep here, but I can't, they'll drag me off to Xiguan, your father, your uncle, your aunt, them, they'll drag me off to Xiguan."

"If you hide here, they won't be able to find you to drag you to Xiguan." The little boy's eyes sparkle, he grabs his grandpa's arm and says: "If you get into the ground and die here, they won't be able to find you, you'll be able to lie here forever, won't you?"

"You can't lie here," the little girl shrieks. "There's no bed, snakes will bite you."

The old man turns to gaze at his grandson and holds the little boy to him as he says: "What did you just say? Get me to go into the ground and then I'll die? That's a good idea, but how'll I get in?

"You'll be buried alive." The little boy blinks his eyes after thinking for a while and goes on in a raised voice: "Being buried alive is when you dig a big hole, put the person in the hole, and then cover them over. You die because you can't breathe, that's the way."

"Clever child." The old man's body trembles, the light in his eyes is dim, his smile seems mournful and helpless. "Such a clever boy," he says, still holding the boy closely as he speaks, "but who will dig such a hole? Your grandpa is too old, he has no strength left for digging. Who would dig me a hole?"

"I'll do it," the little boy says, "I can dig you a hole!"

"I can dig too!" the little girl cries, afraid of being left out.

"You're too small," says the old man, pushing his grandson around a little, at once rubbing his eyes and looking down to speak. "Digging takes a lot of strength, you can't do it."

"Can. I've dug holes before." The little boy leans into his grandpa's ear, uneasily revealing his secret. "Do you remember uncle's lost bellwether? It wasn't really lost. I buried it."

The old man unthinkingly lifts his hand, wanting to seize his grandson's ear but, too fatigued, he lets the hand drop to his knee and says: "Burying a ram and burying a person are not the same thing. A ram is an animal, but your grandpa is a human being, a living human being at that."

"Of course, it's the same with people, you just make the hole a bit bigger, don't you?" says the little boy.

"But how can you bury your own grandpa alive?

Without me there would never have been your father, and there would never have been you. How could you bury your own grandpa alive?" He coughs for a while, then rolls up the hem of his jacket to wipe his eyes, saying: "It's not right. Your father would beat you to death."

"It'll be our secret, they don't need to know." The little boy looks at his sister while saying: "Don't worry about her, she won't say anything, see if I don't beat her to death if she does."

The old man smiles but says no more. He closes his eyes and thinks about what the child has said. His mouth still holds a generous smile, but he knows that tears are falling unbidden from his eyes. He cannot hear the sound of the tears falling, he can only hear the heavy sigh of the earth.

The little boy lifts his hand to the old man's nose and says: "Grandpa, are you still breathing?"

"I'm still breathing, I'm still alive." The old man opens his eyes again, still leaning on the trunk of the tree and says: "Take your sister to go and play over there and don't be too loud. Don't you want to see the white crane? If you're loud, you'll scare it off."

The little boy takes the little girl with him to the other side of the pond to catch loach, standing with her in a newly dug irrigation ditch. They aren't managing to grab another loach, and he does not know by whom, but a pickaxe and spade have been left behind in the ground. Usually, the little boy will not take notice of such things, but this business with the invisible crane and the loach catching is boring him so he picks up the tools, iron pickaxe in one hand, spade in the other, and walks back towards the walnut tree with his voice raised to his sister:

"You don't understand anything, Grandpa's scared of the crematorium, he doesn't want to get burned into a cloud of smoke, he wants to be buried. If you want to bury a person, first you must dig a hole!"

When they arrive at the walnut tree, they find that the old man is asleep, his dreaming face reminds them of the last gourd left over in winter. The siblings stand together in the circle on the ground, looking at him for a while, whispering to each other, then the boy imitates the adults and heaves the pickaxe into the air, taking the first chunk of earth out of the circle on the ground.

The sound of the pickaxe wakes the old man. He opens his eyes: "I told you two not to make a noise, why are you still being so loud? You're going to scare off the white crane."

"There is no white crane," says the little girl. "Grandpa you're tricking us. Daddy says you've got dim eyes now you're old and they've turned geese into cranes."

"The white crane will come." The old man raises his head to the heavens. "The sun is still too high," he says. "Wait for the moon to appear over those mountains, the white crane will come."

The little boy tries to hide the pickaxe behind his back, kicks the shovel underfoot, but he sees that the old man's gaze has found them, suddenly gloomy, yet suddenly bright. The old man stares fixedly at those two tools, taking deep rasping breaths all the while. The boy is seized with panic. "It's you who wanted to be buried," he says, "You can't go telling my dad!"

"I'm not going to tell him." The old man smiles and

lifts his hands to rub the eyes in his lolling head. "I'm muddled from sleep and it made me forget what I told you. It's me who wanted to be buried alive, I don't want to let them take me to the crematorium, I don't want to turn into smoke, I want to stay here and be carried away by the white crane."

"Grandpa did you forget? If you want to be buried alive first you need to dig a hole!" says the little boy.

"First you need to dig a hole, but the hole needs to be very, very big and very, very deep to be able to hide your grandpa's body inside. Could you dig a hole that wide and that deep?" the old man says.

"It doesn't need to be that wide, just really deep. You can stand in it," the little boy says.

"Clever child." The old man looks fondly at his grandson, and at the pickaxe in his hand, and the shovel on the ground. After a while the old man says: "In that case, dig away, lift the pickaxe high, it will be easier. Dig, and if anybody asks you what you're doing, just say you're planting a tree."

The boy responds clearly, lifting the pickaxe once more and saying to his sister: "Step aside, you can't help so just don't get in the way."

The little girl runs to her grandpa and, leaning onto her grandpa's knees and watching her brother dig, she says: "Grandpa don't get buried, if you get buried, you won't be able to breathe, you'll die."

The old man kisses his granddaughter's face. "Clever child," he says. "Your grandpa will die, but death in earth is better than death by fire, death by fire would turn your grandpa into a wisp of smoke, but with death in earth your grandpa will still be able to see the white crane. Your grandpa wants to be carried away by the white crane."

The old man holds the little girl tightly to him as he watches his grandson dig the hole. "Take a little break," he says, "don't tire yourself out, I feel like you could let me have a turn with the shovel myself."

Occasionally someone walks along the path beside the pond and sees the old man beneath the walnut tree, digging a hole with his grandchildren, and assumes that the three of them are planting a tree. They think that this sick old man who has not done farm work for many years still has no choice but to plant trees, then there are others who see the old man taking his grandson and his granddaughter to sit by the edge of the pond, looking all around, and they have heard of this business with the old man and the white crane but have never seen it, so they do not believe it. They chuckle as they say:

"That old man, he's taken his grandchildren to see the white crane, hasn't he!"

Dusk arrives, yet the figure of the white crane does not, the hole beneath the walnut tree is very deep, and the three who dug it are weary. They sit together on the mound of damp, freshly dug earth, looking into the hole at their feet, looking at the weak remaining sunlight casting its rays into the earth through the leaves of the tree, twinkling pieces of shattered gold, warm and mysterious.

The old man wipes sweat from his grandson's forehead, saying: "Look how tired you are. But you don't know how much you've done for your grandpa."

"I'm not tired," says the little boy, "I'm just saving some energy to fill it in."

The old man gets his grandson to listen to the hole's voice. "Do you hear the sound coming from the hole?" he says. "It's the sigh of the earth beneath, the earth sighs all year round."

The little boy lies on his stomach at the edge of the hole for a while as he listens, then raises his head to say: "There's no sigh, there's no sound at all."

"You can't hear it, either." The old man shakes his head and says: "None of you can hear the sighing earth, only I know what it sighs for, and now it sighs for me."

"Grandpa, do you really want to be put in?" The little boy looks at his grandfather's face and says: "Why are you crying? It's you who wanted this, if you don't want to be buried then don't, let's all go home."

"No, I want to get in." The old man slowly gets to his feet, leaning on his grandson's shoulder as he says: "These are tears of happiness. You're so young, and you've helped your grandpa so much. Now, your grandpa really wants to be buried, don't be afraid when it's time to cover me with the soil, you need to seal me in there tight, so they can't find me. Don't be afraid, remember that you're helping me, your grandpa doesn't want to become a wisp of smoke."

"I'm not afraid." The little boy looks at the shovel in his hand as he speaks. "I can just use a shovel, it's easy."

The old man looks towards the empty pool for a while, talking to himself, the sun has fallen behind the mountains, the white crane should come soon. The old man buttons his jacket then turns to his granddaughter to say: "Don't look at your grandpa for a while, watch the pond, you'll see the crane, look, it drinks from the water over there."

The old man slips into the hole, the trio's labour unexpectedly allowing his entire body to fit into the hole. He stands in the hole and turns a gratified and pleased smile toward his grandson, saying: "Good child, now start to fill it in. Remember, one spadeful at a time, and I won't allow you to stop, never stop. Come on, let's start."

Obediently, the boy begins. Other than a few coughs, he no longer hears his grandpa's instructions, but he doesn't need to, he has been told not to stop and so he won't. One spadeful at a time he goes until he sees fresh damp earth black against the white of his grandfather's hair and he hesitates, saying:

"Grandpa, you won't be able to breathe after these next ones."

He hears his grandfather's reply from within the earth, saying:

"Don't stop, keep going. Tell them, I was carried away by the white crane.

The voice from beneath the earth seems to come from faraway, but is still clear. The boy remembers his grandfather's final words, he thinks that if his grandfather can still talk from within the earth, he might still be able to breathe, he says he's going to be carried away by the white crane.

The boy returns home with a shovel in one hand and his little sister's in the other, and as he stands in the doorway knocking dirt from his body, he suddenly becomes afraid and raises his voice to call out to the adults:

"Grandpa's been carried away by the white crane!"

II

Wooden Radio

木壳收音机

Dr Mo held a black cotton umbrella in his hand as he passed beneath the overpass. There was a metallic eruption overhead, and the umbrella's handle shook in his palms while he lowered its canopy, running out from the other side of the bridge as he did so. He looked up to see a black freight train passing along the tracks, its sections either covered by tarpaulin or painted with white codes flashing before his eyes, a breath of wind rolling along beside them as they went.

Dr Mo started with fright.

The rain had already stopped, either that or it had never rained in this northern district of the city at all; this dry stone path didn't have a single trace of rain on it. He folded his umbrella. Odd weather, he thought. It had been raining when he left the home of his patient in the southern district, but now he realised that he knew neither when nor where the deluge had stopped so abruptly.

He kept to the left side of the street. A dog wandered over a hill of garbage on the dock as he watched and, shaking away a few houseflies with his umbrella, he crossed to the right side. It was densely populated with homes, free from the garbage waste. As he passed the Xiri Cotton Store he glimpsed the figure of a woman lying on a bamboo couch through its unlatched door. He did not recognise her and she appeared to be sleeping. Dr Mo saw that she was wearing shorts. So he stopped there for a moment, not anticipating that the woman would turn over and, her eyes still heavy with sleep, spew out a stream of appalling language.

Dr Mo started with fright. He picked up his feet and started to move, a gloomy and agitated feeling descending on him for the rest of his journey home.

A key is fastened to a keyring, the keyring is fastened to a keychain, the keychain is fastened to a loop on Dr Mo's belt. Standing at the door to his home, Dr Mo anxiously searched for the copper horse's head which branded that key. He owned two keys with the same feature, and so could never distinguish between the one which opened his front door from the one which opened the door to his clinic. He went about trying each of them in turn as usual, but this time he was startled to hear movement coming from the roof of his house.

"Who is on my roof?" He stepped back a few paces, standing on tiptoes and straining to see above the wall. The clucking tap of a few broken tiles accompanied a wave of dust which fell from the gable. Dr Mo shielded his eyes and, still facing upwards, repeated: "Who is on my roof? Answer me or I'll call for somebody."

Call for who? The faces of two bricklayers appeared above the eaves one after the other. The one surnamed Sun used his trowel to knock on the leaky iron drainpipe. The one surnamed Li pulled out a fern from between the tiles. Li said: "See how he's trying to hurry us? Forget about it, who would want to be up here sunbathing in this heat anyway?"

"Why are you on my roof?" shouted Dr Mo, lifting his head.

"We're fixing your leak," said Sun, "Didn't you report that your roof was broken? We've been busy here all morning, haven't even had a drop to drink."

"Leak? I don't have any leak, why are you fixing a leak?" Dr Mo didn't know what was going on. "You must be mistaken," he said. "I didn't make any such report, there is no leak."

"You're Seventeen Toon Street, aren't you? You're not Deng Laixian?"

It certainly was a mistake. Dr Mo sighed and pointed northwards. "This is seven, seventeen is over there, next to the chemical plant. Hurry up and get over there."

The people on the roof said: "We'll just stop to rest a little, we're so tired."

"Since you're tired," said Dr Mo after a moment's consideration, "have a rest." He entered his home and closed the door hard behind him. Inside, the floor was glazed with the dampness which marked the rainy season. Dr Mo discovered that his floor, table and chair were now coated with mud, hairy with dirt, and that the clock which had been in his family for years leant askance on his wall. His state of mind became all the more glowering and odious. It was all because of those two bricklayers, inexplicably up on his roof.

Dr Mo twisted the dial of his wooden radio. Music came from its speakers, music which Dr Mo knew by heart and music which, when concluded, would signal the beginning of the weather report: weather condition, maximum and minimum temperature, wind direction and wind speed. He had listened to this same information for so many years that he could recite it backwards. Dr Mo sat in his mahogany chair and waited for the familiar sound of the reporter's mellow, soothing voice. The wooden radio's music stopped abruptly; a change marked by the rustling crackle of a magnetic disk. Her voice came smoothly as always, talking without pause, but when she came to announce the maximum and minimum temperatures Dr Mo cried out in surprise.

"Today's high will be twenty-five degrees, while the low will reach thirty-one," she said.

Dr Mo heard his own astonished voice resounding

around the stifling room as he stood up from his mahogany chair, the sound falling somewhere between delight and horror. He bent to inspect the radio. "Wrong, you said it wrong." Dr Mo tapped the radio, but the announcer knew nothing about it. To repeat that, her voice came again from the radio: "Today's high will be twenty-five degrees, while the low will reach thirty-one."

"No, it will not. She's talking nonsense." Dr Mo turned the volume down and went to stand on the stone step at the back of his house. He began to wash himself in the basin which lay there. The river gurgled at his feet. A smell of ammonia fertilizer floated above its moss-green waters as it ran through the city carrying grease, dead rats and plastics which would protrude spasmodically from its surface. Dr Mo poured a basin of water over his head, his eyes following the erratic path marked by those dislodged suds on the stone as they sought to merge with the river's flow.

There was a railway bridge which spanned the river's width a hundred metres away, quiet then in the relative early afternoon peace of a road with nothing to speed along behind its diamond railings. Dr Mo looked at the distant bridge, twisting his towel in both hands. The radio had changed programmes, now it played the beginning of the classic tale *Lin Chong Flees in the Night*. The storyteller's voice undulated as they spoke, and Dr Mo listened to the innumerable words of their old-fashioned *tanci* storytelling as he rubbed the towel over his body. Master Lin burned the fodder depot to the ground and headed straight for Liang-shan Park through the wind and snow. Dr Mo smiled and made a contemptuous, obscene gesture towards the radio on his table.

"You're all talking gibberish," he said. Master Lin was guarding the fodder depot.

The doctor's home, which he occupied alone, overlooked the Donglin River. It was his custom to return to it every day for an afternoon nap and to listen to the radio as he slept. Sometimes he would listen conscientiously to that afternoon's programming. Sometimes he thought about honeysuckle and skullcap root medicine. Sometimes he thought about our pink organs and the bacteria which squirm among them. Sometimes he thought about nothing, and quickly fell asleep. The room was completely empty but for the wooden radio on the table. Dr Mo would sleep on the bed, the floor, or simply on the table as long as he could fall asleep easily. Other than when he slept, the doctor could hear his heartbeat ticking with the abruptness of that clock on the wall. When he slept he heard nothing at all.

But Dr Mo was not asleep. The two bricklayers had still not descended from the roof and the sound of them clacking away on the green tile was sharp, grating and irregular. Dr Mo did not know why they were staying up there for so long. He could see their swaying shadows through the glass of the dormer window above him. They will come down any moment, he thought, there is no need to press them, any moment now they will be down. The thought was crossing his mind that they cannot just stay up there on my roof for no reason at the very moment that he saw the dormer window go dark. It was as if somebody had covered it with newspaper and then put something on top, and then there was the sound of a heavy object falling on the glass. What are they doing now? The doctor sat up from his straw mat and went to stand on the table, raising his face to the window until he could finally make out that the somethings on top of the newspaper were in fact pieces of crockery and a bottle. Are they eating and drinking on my roof? He seized a bamboo pole and set to poking at the glass.

"Come down at once, what are you playing at drinking on my roof?"

The two bricklayers on the roof did not stir. Dr Mo, supposing that perhaps a radio sounding out from one of the other roofs was masking his voice, took the bamboo pole to his back door and used it to knock at the tiles there.

"Come down. Aren't you going to seventeen to fix their leak? What are you doing up there drinking on my roof?"

"We're not going to seventeen, we're having some beer. We're thirsty," said Li.

"Come and have some, you'd better bring a glass though," said Sun.

"I'm trying to have my nap. If you want to drink then come down, drink wherever you want, just not on my roof." Dr Mo used the pole to whack the tiles again as he raised his voice to say: "I really don't understand why you would want to drink your beer on my roof!"

"You have your sleep, we'll have our drink. Don't be such a meddler," said Sun.

"But you're up on my roof, it's too loud," said Dr Mo.

"Who says it's your roof? The room is yours, but the rooftop isn't. That's not private," said Li with a sneer. "We do maintenance, we know about this stuff."

"This is gibberish." Dr Mo reddened as he spoke. "I've never heard such gibberish." He wanted to say something else but found himself at a loss for words. He took the bamboo pole back into the room and let out a filthy curse. So quickly, he thought to himself, the appalling language of that cotton-shop woman is being used by me. But seeing as he was so very angry, he reasoned, he could not really be blamed.

Dr Mo lay back down on his straw mat, listening to the story's finale on the radio. He could not help but feel that this afternoon's rest had been a total defeat. He had neither slept nor got any of the week's cases in order. And then his hateful mood brought repulsive things to mind. Eczema and piles, urinary incontinence and swelling of the prostate - all flicking before his eyes like rotten stewed vegetables.

It was approximately two in the afternoon when someone hurriedly knocked at Dr Mo's door. He opened his door to see a woman in a grey skirt with a boy of about ten years old behind her. He recalled that the boy was one of his patients, one whom he saw with his mother almost every month on account of his kidney problems. It was his refusal to have injections which brought them to Dr Mo, a doctor of Chinese medicine who had never injected a patient.

The boy subconsciously shook the woman in the grey skirt's hand away as she led him softly along. In his own fingers, the doctor noticed, he held a windmill made from coloured paper and sticks of wood; red, yellow and blue, three colours all together. It became resplendent in the midst of the interior's gloom.

"I've been knocking a while, were you asleep?" the woman asked after she entered.

"Didn't you hear that noise up on the roof? Can you guess who it is? Two bricklayers. They're drinking beer up there. They say that one's roof is not a person's private property."

"His urine is bad, it's yellow and murky. I took him to the hospital, they said that his red blood cells have got two pluses." After hesitating a while the woman said: "I'm worried to death."

"What did you say?" As if waking from a dream, Dr Mo reached to take the child's hand which was deftly twisted out of his way. The child puffed up his cheeks to blow a gust of air towards the windmill. It rotated once, feebly, before stopping. Dr Mo grabbed for the child's hand again and this time he caught it. "Don't dodge," said Dr Mo. "How am I to heal you if I can't feel your pulse?" He held his breath to feel the child's pulse but his eyes were drawn to the bright, dazzling blades of the windmill in that other hand. A weak and lethargic feeling suddenly came over him.

"I really don't understand," he said. "How can the child still be ill after so many proper medications?" The woman ruffled her boy's precious hair.

"I'm really worried sick," she said.

"Could it be that the child has been secretly eating salt? I did tell you not to let him take any, otherwise my medications won't work."

"I'm really worried sick." Her voice suddenly became mute and gloomy, and she didn't say a word in response to the doctor's question but asked her own in response: "Is there any way you can get the child to eat salt? Adults not eating any salt isn't right, never mind such a little child."

Dr Mo smiled a little, thinking the woman had become muddled. He said: "Aren't you treating the child's illness? Once he is cured, he may eat salty food, but while he is being treated we have to avoid it. You cannot make him eat salt."

"Just a little. I want to make him more energetic."

Dr Mo sighed, suddenly filled with indignance but knowing that it would be inappropriate to show it. He felt that he was wasting his breath on this woman, so he turned to the child and said: "Do you want to get better? If so, you can't eat any salt."

"No," said the boy, "I'm going to."

"No?" Dr Mo smiled again and bent to the child's ear. "Could it be that you're not afraid to die?"

"I won't die. I'm only ten. You're going to die. You're going to die soon."

Dr Mo started with fright, releasing the child's scrawny wrist.

"Let me see your tongue," he said, pretending not to have heard what the boy had said. He used a sterilised chip of wood to pry open the child's teeth, roughly, and the boy cried out in a shrill tone.

"Be gentle," said the woman in the skirt, her voice discontented. "The child doesn't understand." Dr Mo shook his head, thinking, yes, the child doesn't understand. But as a mother you cannot dote on them in all things. But then he thought that there really is no point in being angry with a sick child, and so he turned to the woman with a more jovial voice and said:

"Did you hear the weather forecast earlier today? The reporter said that we would have a high of twenty-five degrees with a low of thirty-one." Dr Mo smiled as he spoke, saying: "It was really funny. She said it twice – and both times were wrong."

"I don't listen to the weather." Then casually she added: "I don't have spare time to listen." Her eyes moved to the wooden radio on the table. There was no programming, but the red pilot light was on. If one listened very carefully, one could still hear the low hum of an electrical current around it. "There's no programme," the woman said. "Why do you still have the radio on?"

"I always listen to the radio whenever I'm at home, and the news will begin soon. I switch it off at nine o'clock." Dr Mo bent over his table to write a new prescription which he stuffed into the woman's hand. "Try this new medicine," he said. "Perhaps he'll recover very soon. Be absolutely sure not to let him touch a drop of salt, otherwise he'll never get better."

The woman had already stood up and was leading the child to the door by his hand when she stopped suddenly to fix Dr Mo with an attentive look, seeming as if she had stopped herself from saying something. Her son, meanwhile, had shaken off her hand. One of his feet was already outside while the other was still within Dr Mo's threshold.

"I don't want to play with this windmill any more, you have it." The child threw the toy into Dr Mo's house as he spoke. The doctor saw it tumble, broken and soundless, onto the floor. It looked like a gliding tropical bird.

"Your complexion doesn't look so good," said the woman finally. "Do you have heart disease? Certainly, you must have heart disease!"

Dr Mo was startled. He didn't know what had given this woman cause to judge that he had heart disease, and more to the point, it was she that had come to ask him for medical help. Dr Mo paid attention to the woman's expression, finding it a touch sly and vengeful in appearance.

"Heart disease?" He subconsciously touched his chest

above his heart as he spoke. "Maybe a little, but it can't be serious. I can treat myself."

"Take care," said the woman, pulling her child away a few more steps before calling out that final sentence to Dr Mo.

Half of the street was scattered with golden sunlight, the other half shaded by the eaves of buildings above. Dr Mo stood at his doorway, watching those two walking away as a feeling of apprehension arose in him. "Take care." He rolled the woman's words over and over in his mind when something came crashing down from his roof – a beer bottle. It smashed into shards of glass as it collided with the floor, a heavy alcoholic scent emerging from between its shattered pieces. Dr Mo made an effort to see up to his roof but was unable to make anything out. The only thing he could say for certain was that those two bricklayers were still up there, drinking. He opened his mouth wide, wanting to shout something up at them but finding that his throat had dried into glue. The realisation was followed by pain. His head began to swim. There is nothing for it, just let them drink, see how long they can go for. The doctor went back into his room and closed the door. He felt that there had been some change in his body, and he wanted to check his blood pressure before he went about discerning the cause.

Dr Mo sat at his catalpa wood table, wrapping the cuff of the blood pressure monitor several times around his arm before tightening it. He held up the monitor gauge to check his own reading. A musical prelude started to emerge from the wooden radio on the table, signalling to him that the news would begin shortly. The doctor believed that the music would not interfere with his results, but the mercury just kept rising. He could no longer hear the ticking, the sound so familiar to him. Dr Mo began to panic; can my blood pressure really be at the highest limit? His head was heavy. His weak shoulders, his neck and his spine could no longer support his head. He sat on the chair, slowly caving in with a tilt to his right. The last thing Dr Mo saw were the blades of the child's discarded windmill rotating naturally at his feet. On that afternoon, wind whipped from the surface of the river beneath his window, the windmill's colourful blades rotated with a rustle in the soft breeze.

Dusk came, and a rousing march blared from the radio in Dr Mo's house. The noise disturbed the drunken sleep of the two bricklayers above, who thought that it had been going on for quite some time. It practically deafened them. Li climbed to the edge of the roof only to discover that somebody had taken their stepladder.

"The ladder's disappeared somewhere, how are we going to get down? said Li.

"Just jump," was Sun's dazed reply.

Li asked again: "Jump from where?"

"From the lowest point, obviously," said Sun.

Li selected the eaves to the back of the house. The wall was not too tall there, and on the ground beneath them lay a basket full of cabbage and a red plastic spittoon. Li first bent at the waist and then jumped, landing perfectly in the soft vegetables with no discomfort at all. Li shouted happily before lifting the bamboo screen at the back of Dr Mo's house. He entered immediately.

"Coming through, I need to get to the street." As Li passed Dr Mo, he patted his shoulder affectionately. The doctor did not stir.

"What are you still angry with us for?" said Li. "We've come down, haven't we?"

Dr Mo still didn't move. Now Li noticed the blood pressure machine on the table. How can you take your own blood pressure? Li dragged the electrical wire as he walked, pulling both machine and man onto the floor as he did. He realised that something was wrong.

"Quick, there's something up with him!"

Li ran to the stone step at the back door where he saw Sun, who must have scooped up some of Dr Mo's soap from the window, as he was standing waist-deep in the river washing his hair. Li watched Sun. His head was white for a while, then black for a while. Li watched Sun spread the soap over his head again and again, sinking into the water each time. Sun was ignoring his call.

Even though the water was so dirty and foul, Sun was quite content with his bath. He saw a wooden boat heading from the upper reaches of the river, piled high with cotton and grain. A young woman was punting the boat along with a pole, while the sculler was an even younger woman. The bricklayer Sun felt indescribably happy and waved his damp shirt in the boat's direction.

"Where are you going?" Sun cried out to them.

"To Changshu," the women onboard replied.

III

Watermelon Boats

西瓜船

ALMOST ALL THE WATERMELON BOATS come from Song Keng. They are recognisable to the people who live at the water's edge by their shape, bigger and slenderer than the dark-wood Shaoxing boats, and their wooden bodies fitted with an iron sheet close to the water's brim. Their canopies are distinctive too, made out of thatched wheat stalks piled onto four wooden poles rather than tarpaulin, making them look like shockproof sheds during an earthquake.

The scorching July heat does the watermelon sellers' advertising for them. In the northern part of the city, people would spend their evenings pushing bikes loaded with burlap sacks or nylon bags over to Tiexin Bridge where the Song Keng boats were moored. Greedy, sharp-eyed children watching from their river-facing windows would be the first to spot them as the earliest of the boats emerged from the midst of the brewery wharf's shipping vessels. "The watermelon boats have come," they would say while stamping their feet at the adults. "Quick, let's get some!" There are also those like the fool Guangchun who run ahead of the boats, shouting as they lead them to the bridge: "The watermelon boats are coming! The watermelons have come!"

They arrived from Song Keng year after year, changing only in quantity. All the children could recognise them immediately with those thatched wheat mats and their makeshift cooking stoves billowing out smoke. Together, they made it seem like a shanty town had descended to cover the surface of the river.

Country men are hard workers, but the watermelon sellers' behaviour once they had arrived at Tiexing Bridge might make you doubt it. They were Song Keng men of all ages, gathering together to play cards or nesting in their own pile of watermelons to doze when they had no buyers, waking up and slowly making their way out of the canopy if somebody came to the boat. They typically wore long-sleeved white shirts and grey-blue trousers which, their wearers unused to leather belts, were held up by bolts of blue cotton. The older they were, the less they cared about their appearance, the oldest among them left their trousers hanging open so you could see the colour of their underwear beneath. They all had shoes: military boots, rain boots, cloth shoes, and some of the younger ones even had pairs made of leather. Despite this, they all left them discarded in the cabin as they walked around barefoot. Overall, their appearance gave one the impression of being improperly dressed regardless of the fact that they were wearing more clothing than the people on the street. It had already been many years since they first came to Tiexing Bridge with their wares and, as the years went on, the people on the street had become accustomed to calling them by name. With a friendly slap on the shoulder as they climbed onto the boat, they would try to use their familiarity to secure a discount. Some of them would even bring along a four-penny iced bean treat as they came, a Toon Street resident scheme to which the people on the boats would react with a smile on their face and a glint in their eye, saying: "You'd better pick your melons out quick. The rains were no good this year, so they haven't grown well. Just these few boats and in two days we'll have all sold out."

There are no platform scales on the boats, their owners use the old-fashioned method with those hanging scales which need two people to lift the watermelons on a shoulder pole. If everybody's hands were full, a seller would step over from another boat to help. The sound of people haggling rang out over the swaying decks, people voicing their side of the dispute like two ambassadors engaged in diplomacy. You give a little here, I give a little there, until an agreement is reached. It was in such a way that the Song Keng watermelons departed from their boats, and it was in such a way that one Song Keng watermelon in particular found a home in Chen Suzhen's basket.

Chen Suzhen visited the watermelon boats just about every other day from July until August when their supply gradually ran dry, knowing that her son Shoulai loved to eat them. She was a serious haggler who would buy her daily watermelon only after its sweetness and ripeness had been guaranteed with a pat, but each one of them was so large and round that she could not have guessed that, when she used all her strength to heave this one over her shoulder, she was really hauling a basket of calamity into her home.

This happened many years ago, so nobody really remembers the particulars of the purchase itself. I only remember that she had bought a big watermelon, but that it was unripe. You cannot tell from the outside when they are like that; white on the inside and no good to eat, but they are still watermelons. Naturally, this kind of mistake happens all the time and is easy to resolve. There are two options, you can either eat the white melon as if it were radish or, if you are not worried about the hassle, just take it back to Tiexing Bridge and change it for a new ripe one.

Chen Suzhen chose the second option. Typical of Toon Street's women, she was the bustling sort who went about wishing she could do two things with one hand, and so she had plenty of other household duties to attend to on the same journey that she used to exchange the melon. Her basket was filled with cruet and rice wine, and on top of that she had to go to the cloth store and fetch some pyjama fabric for the tailor. She simply could not carry the basket with the water-melon inside, so she lifted it back out. But words are cheap, and she knew that. So, taking up a spoon, she used the utensil to scoop out a chunk of white flesh and secured it within a wrap of oil paper to use as her evidence that it was inedible.

When Chen Suzhen arrived at Tiexing Bridge with her basket, she found that two of the three boats had already gone. The boat which was left was the one which belonged to Fu San. Fu San's boat happened to be the one that she usually frequented, but there had been so many people crowding around Lao Zhang's boat that morning that she had gone to join the fun. She never would have expected Lao Zhang to be gone by the end of the day. Since he never could have sold out of melons so quickly, she guessed that they were all unripe, and so he had gone to sell them elsewhere. As she stood under the end of the bridge with the oil-paper wrapped melon in her hand, an intense dislike of the Song Keng people came over Chen Suzhen. Hate in your heart will out through your mouth, and so she called out to him; sweet this, ripe that, country folk are always cheating people!

She saw now that only Fu San remained on his boat; the other youngster with him had gone who knows where. Chen Suzhen did not know how to write Fu San's name, but she could call it out. Her impression of Fu San was that he was the quietest of the Song Keng people, and among those who do not speak much there are two types; the honest and the cunning. Chen Suzhen didn't know which of these categories he fell into, but she went towards his boat prepared to denounce those on the other whether he passed the message on to them or not. There was also the matter of watermelon quality. Chen Suzhen felt obliged to represent the interests of the Toon Street citizenry when she gave the warning:

"If you have this many unripe melons next year, don't bother to come and sell them here; you're better off keeping them in Song Keng and feeding them to the pigs." When she got to the side of Fu San's boat and saw him emerge from the cabin with a red melon in his hands, the idea came to her to take the first strike and put him in a position which she had not before intended.

"Fu San, Fu San, I've been buying melons from you for how many years, and you give me a white one?"

Fu San ate the melon in his hand, traces of straw still clearly visible on his cheek from his recent nap. Chen Suzhen jumped in front of him. "You keep the good ones for yourself and sell the unripe ones!"

Fu San looked into her basket. There was cruet, rice wine, a pile of pickled vegetables and a wrap of oil paper. He picked up one of the vegetables and popped it into his mouth with a smile but didn't say a word.

"You ungrateful man," she said, "you've given me an unripe melon."

He turned his head and spat the vegetable into the water. "Too sour," he said, "no good." He looked back to her and said nothing more.

"Are you mute? OK then, fine by me, I don't want to listen to you anyway, I want to see you getting to work. Go and fetch me a good melon."

Chen Suzhen watched as he placed the triangular

sections of leftover peel from his melon on the canopy one at a time.

"Are you drying them out," she asked. "Do you pickle them or fry them?"

"We pickle them, you'd need oil to fry them." Then he turned his head and said: "That white melon? How am I supposed to exchange it if you haven't brought it with you?

"I couldn't carry it," she said as she took the oil paper out of her basket. "It was a big one. I've scooped some out, you'll know I couldn't eat it as soon as you see it."

Fu San looked at the oil paper, at the melon, and then at her face. When his eyes met hers he smiled, saying: "I didn't know you could be so shrewd, trying to exchange a scoop of melon for a whole one."

Bewildered by the smile, Chen Suzhen said: "That's my evidence, OK? I've been buying watermelon on your boat for how many years and now you shut me out?"

Fu San kept smiling, but his expression was cold. "If you bought a no-good chicken, could you pluck one of its feathers to exchange it for a good one? Woman," he said, "you think that country folk are all fools. There are plenty of you on the street, but I still remember which boat you bought that melon on. Do you think I don't know? An exchange is an exchange, but paper for a melon is the world's best bargain!"

Chen Suzhen felt that Fu San had allowed her to walk into this trap, making her feel both extremely awkward and surprised that he was so astute. You cannot judge a man by his appearance alone, and she had misjudged Fu San. Nonetheless, she was the kind of woman filled with so much self-respect that any damage to it would cause her to become quite angry.

"I've misjudged you, Fu San!" she said with an embarrassed laugh. "So this is Fu San, looking so honest, I would never have expected you to be like this." She threw the oil paper into the river and said: "If you don't want to change it then don't change it. You country folk, all swindlers."

Chen Suzhen left the boat empty-handed, so empty in fact that she had even forgotten that she had brought something with her. "Big sister," Fu San chided as he used his punting pole to return her basket to her, "you shouldn't speak like that about country folk. Without country folk you'd be eating air for dinner every day."

"I'm not cursing country folk," replied Chen Suzhen as she took the basket from the pole. "I'm cursing those who bring unripe melons to cheat people."

Standing on the boat, Fu San said: "It's not us cheating people, it's the year's rain. What can we do when the melons are bad?"

"Your melons are bad," she carried on in a fit of rage, "and you still bring them here? Better keep them there and feed them to the pigs. Just you wait and see, you think anybody will fall for it next year?"

The whole thing should have ended there. According to what the people of Toon Street know about Shoulai's mother, it would have been great if the watermelon was exchanged, but no great loss had it not. She was concerned about her reputation, and didn't have a particularly good constitution, but she still wouldn't have caused trouble over a watermelon. However, the watermelon was not for Chen Suzhen. She had bought it for her son, the flesh was his to eat and only whatever he left on the rind would be for her. So, while Chen Suzhen would have resigned herself to misfortune, Shoulai's opinion was another matter entirely.

Shoulai was seventeen that year, and everybody remembers how he would always walk around with a wrinkled brow and a sideways glance as if he were always being mistreated – but who would dare? It was he that bullied the other boys, and even some innocent animals. He was not yet a murderer, but he had already been known to kill cats and dogs. "It won't be long," somebody had said, "before he's killed a person." But we need not mention hindsight for now.

When Shoulai went home that day, he saw the melon sliced in half and soaking in a basin on the table as usual. He noticed that it was white, but roared when he had scooped some into his mouth: "It's unripe! Is this a watermelon or a wax gourd?"

"I went to change it," said Chen Suzhen, busying herself about the kitchen, "but Lao Zhang's boat had already gone, and that Fu San wouldn't change it for me. You'll have to make do, it's only like eating gourd! That Fu San isn't as honest as he looks. I took the melon with me and he still wouldn't change it. He's as shrewd as a ghost. Those Song Keng country folk," she opined, speaking quickly and with the tone of one airing a grievance, never ready to take a loss. Chen Suzhen was used to talking like this to herself in the kitchen, putting right more or less all the things on her mind the whole time she was cooking. She never poured her heart out to her son because he never listened, nor did he ever listen when she tried to teach him how to behave. She was voluble about the benefits of being thrifty to him and he never listened to that, either.

She had no idea that her son would listen to her now,

when her criticism was all just about a watermelon. Unbeknownst to his mother, who did not hear her son's cursing outside, Shoulai had picked up the watermelon and left. She had been frying soybeans with pickled vegetables, she would tell the neighbours afterwards. She never even knew that he had gone out. When she was putting the beans into a bowl, one of them somehow dropped onto the floor. It was just then that a neighbour's child rushed in with the news:

"Shoulai's stabbed somebody on a watermelon boat!"

This time she took her journey to Tiexing Bridge at a run, having to stop to catch her breath on account of her poor constitution. As she squatted there, trying to recover her strength, the wasted time made her so angry that she lifted her fist and began to beat the ground with the object it carried. Many of us still remember that, the thing she was carrying, it wasn't anything special, just a little spatula.

Regarding Fu San's death, the person with the most right to speak is Wang Deji. He works at the agricultural machinery factory. Wang Deji was pushing his bicycle from Tiexing Bridge just in time to see Shoulai fleeing onto it like a frightened hare.

"Move!" said Shoulai, shoving the man and the bicycle which was in his way. The children may have been afraid of Shoulai, but Wang Deji was not. He was just about to curse him out when he felt something wet and syrupy on his shoulder; he knew at a glance that it was blood.

"Shoulai, Shoulai stay there!"

Shoulai didn't listen, he just kept running madly over the

bridge. His plastic shoes carried him as fast as if he had been walking on coals.

"Shoulai, have you stabbed somebody?" Wang Deji called to the boy from the top of the bridge. "You're running like you've stabbed somebody!"

Shoulai didn't listen. In the blink of an eye he was down from the bridge and, with a pause to pull up his athletics trousers, he shouted back to Wang Deji: "He went for me first!" He wiped his hands and ran. In a flash, he had disappeared from Toon Street.

Wang Deji spoke to himself as he followed the trail of blood. "It looks like he's stabbed someone, so much blood!" He saw Fu San the moment he got down from the bridge, swaying as he climbed ashore with a watermelon knife in his hands. Crying women and gaping children came along by his side.

That watermelon boatman Fu San, leaving a trail of blood as he walked, stopped moving when he reached the public toilets, where he bent his waist to rest his head against the wall. He turned an indignant look toward Wang Deji.

"It's you?" Wang Deji was courageous to approach somebody so soaked in gore. "Aren't you the Fu San who sells watermelons?" Fu San's whole body was covered in blood and, leaning against the wall, his body was trembling as he made a great effort to lift the watermelon knife.

"Why are you holding that knife?" said Wang Deji.

"Give it to Xiao Liang," said Fu San.

"Give it to Xiao Liang for what?" asked Wang Deji. "To stab Shoulai?"

Fu San shook his head, then nodded, opening his eyes to look at Wang Deji, still holding that knife aloft. Wang Deji suddenly understood that he wanted him to take the knife. He shook his head.

"I can't take that, how can I help you stab Shoulai? Can't worry about that now, I'm taking you to hospital."

At first, the warm-hearted Wang Deji wanted to carry Fu San on his bicycle, but the bleeding man simply could not do it; he fell every time he tried to sit. Wang Deji held onto his handlebars for a while and, realising that it was no good, locked up his bike and leant it against the wall saying:

"You've lost too much blood for the bike, you don't have the strength, I'll carry you."

And so, it was Wang Deji who carried Fu San from Tiexing Bridge. Wang Deji was strong, running so fast with somebody on his back. When he reached the top of the bridge he saw Chen Suzhen and her spatula, white faced and running towards him.

"What," he shouted to her, "is the use of you running over here? Your son's already brought disaster!"

Chen Suzhen half squatted, breathing heavily as she tried to identify the person on Wang Deji's back. "It's Fu San isn't it, is it serious?"

"What do you mean is it serious?" said Wang Deji. "His blood is pouring onto the street and you ask me if it's serious?" Wang Deji had thought that she would help him, but when she saw them come down from the bridge covered in blood she just cried out and became paralysed, after all women cannot stand the sight of blood, and she was the culprit's mother. As she cried out, Wang Deji heard a clank on the ground behind him – Fu San had dropped his knife just at the place where it would roll to Chen Suzhen's feet.

"Do you want me to pick it up?" he asked Fu San. "It's evidence, we don't want somebody to go off with it."

Fu San didn't understand and asked Wang Deji: "Are you Xiao Liang?"

"I'm not Xiao Liang, I'm Wang Deji from the agricultural machinery factory, don't you recognise me? We met each other at the grocery store two days ago, you broke a bottle of grain liquor, right?"

"You're not Xiao Liang?" said Fu San. "Where the hell is he?"

"How should I know? Said Wang Deji. "Do you remember where he's gone? You've lost too much blood, is your head still clear?"

"My head is clear, it's just that I can't move. Xiao Liang's gone to buy soap. You're not Xiao Liang, I thought it was Xiao Liang carrying me."

"If your head's fine that's good, that'll be the most important thing. Forget about Xiao Liang, it doesn't matter who's carrying you. Carrying you to hospital, saving your life!"

The boys on the street chased after Wang Deji.

"Who is it?" they asked. "Who is it?" The adults all stood shocked in their own doorways, commenting thoughtlessly.

"Another gang fight? What a state it has got to!" When they passed the grocery store, Wang Deji shouted for Xiao Liang.

"Has Xiao Liang come to buy soap?" The girls who worked in the store came out and saw the bleeding man. They didn't know who Xiao Liang was, they just wanted to see who Wang Deji was carrying and make some suggestions to him, saying:

"Wang Deji, why are you carrying him and running, why aren't you calling an ambulance?"

"Do I look like I have six arms and three heads? How am I supposed to call an ambulance with him on my back?"

There were many people on the street, but Xiao Liang was not one of them. Looking for help, Wang Deji's cold eyes found Fatty Xie sitting among a group of people playing chess at the mouth of Taohua Lane. Fatty Xie was also a warm-hearted man, but once he sat down to the chess board, he was indifferent to anything else. His head appeared through the cracks in the crowd and then disappeared again. Wang Deji became incensed and gave up looking for help. In the end, it was simply he alone that took him to the hospital.

Fu San became like a piece of luggage, dangling quietly from Wang Deji's back as he ran. Occasionally he would twitch like somebody with malaria, and then he would be still again. Wang Deji says that all he felt was the other man getting heavier and heavier. Carrying someone that big, both sides need to readjust, but eventually the blood stuck Fu San to Wang Deji's back like glue.

"Come on, come on." Wang Deji says that he did not stop talking the whole way. "Come on," he repeated, "come on, hold on." He was encouraging Fu San, and also encouraging himself. In the end, Wang Deji really did hold on, but Fu San could not. Wang Deji told everybody that when he passed a cement delivery lorry on Beida Bridge, the driver refused to help him save Fu San. When he cursed at him the driver argued back, responding with the political slogan that, by *grasping revolution and promoting production*, he was in fact doing more than Wang Deji to save the people.

Wang Deji doesn't know why Fu San didn't make it to

the end. He ran fast enough. He will not say that he ran faster than an ambulance, but he had certainly been faster than a bike could have been. They arrived quickly at the door of the Fifth People's Hospital, and so did that man named Xiao Liang from Song Keng.

"Who did it, who did it?" he shouted to Wang Deji. A useless village man, all he could do was cry.

It was too much for Wang Deji, who cried out:

"First I save a man and then I have to turn one in?"

His iron strength gave out. He helped Fu San onto Xiao Liang's back and stumbled to lean against a wall. He vomited, vomited again, and discovered that Xiao Liang was still standing there crying. Angry, he pushed at him and shouted:

"Stop your useless bullshit crying and go, go!" But when Wang Deji pushed Xiao Liang, he discovered what a state Fu San was really in. His eyes gazed angrily to heaven, but the expression was frozen. Truly courageous, Wang Deji used his finger to pry open the watermelon seller's eye and peered in – the pupil was already huge. That useless Xiao Liang rushed into the hospital reception room with Fu San on his back.

"Quick doctor," he wailed to a door guard, "quick, help him!"

On the matter of Fu San's death, whatever Wang Deji said is written here. That year, the youth of Toon Street all approached him to recall the details of that journey over and over. Frankly speaking, some people just have a taste for gore. However, Wang Deji himself had good judgement and whenever he told the story, he emphasised the hardship of trying to save a life and the regret of having failed. This all happened years ago. Forgive my old-fashioned nature but I have to consider the possibility that this story might have a negative impact on my young readers. Fu San's body lying in the morgue of the Fifth People's Hospital produced all kinds of ripples, but I have decided to describe that part of it no further.

To return to the boats, the first thing to say is concerning that other man, Xiao Liang.

Xiao Liang is a useless man, a bit dim. This is not something for which we need to rely on Wang Deji's testament as evidence, everyone could see it plainly. When the local police had put up a sign that prohibited persons unrelated to the investigation from entering the boat, one of them certainly explained to Xiao Liang that this included him, and that it was in order to preserve the crime scene. However, he had only a hazy comprehension of what they had said and, as he was pushed from cabin to prow and from prow to shore, his face showed an expression of perplexed obedience, as if of a sleepwalker. When the police left, he began to cry, to shout after them:

"Have you caught the criminal?"

That night, after the police were all gone, more personnel arrived to carry on with their own meticulous inspection of the crime scene for no real reason. They saw Xiao Liang sitting on the shore, hugging his knees and getting in people's way, so much so that some encouraged him to go back to bed on the boat just to get rid of him. These people were punished by the public security officers, whose uniforms drew unanimous hatred.

"They don't know shit." This was said after they had left. "They can deal with prostitutes and punks but they'll muddle a murder. What do we need fingerprinting for? So many people saw Shoulai stab him, what more evidence do we need? Get to sleep back on your own boat, no problem. How can you be prohibited?"

Others gave him different advice: "The public bathroom has just been opened. Give the old man who watches the door a watermelon and he'll let you sleep in there."

Other people disagreed with them, saying: "Are you stupid? Can't you see he can't leave the boat? It still has melons on it, he has to watch them."

Xiao Liang looked at San Ba and his chums with mistrust, they seemed the kind of shifty individuals who would undoubtedly be harbouring hidden intentions behind any sudden display of concern. He was also afraid of them. He eyed them cautiously, moving around here and there to give them room.

"I'm just sleeping here," he said, "keeping an eye on my boat." Then he withdrew and covered his head to get back to sleep. He listened as he slept to San Ba and the others discussing Shoulai and, on discovering that Shoulai was not a friend of this crowd, raised his voice to admonish him. "All this for a melon, killing a man for a melon. The life of a country man is worth as much as a melon?"

Soon the entire city had heard about the watermelon incident and, owing to the fact that the murderer and the murdered could not hang around to satisfy people's curiosity, everyone came rushing to see the sealed-up boat and the blood which remained sparingly on the prow and the shore.

Xiao Liang became braver in the daylight. People would look at the boat, and he would look at them.

"We Song Keng people are coming," he would say. "They're already on the way." They knew what he meant; they were going to retaliate. "Shoulai has already been cuffed," they told him. "He was waiting for a train, but he was too impatient and went to the culture centre near the station to watch their videos. He was arrested the moment he sat down. So, everything's fine then?"

"The life," said Xiao Liang, "the life of a country man is worth a watermelon?"

"Shoulai's family have told us," somebody said, "that since he's only seventeen he'll go to a juvenile detention centre, he won't be executed."

"You're kidding me," shouted Xiao Liang. "Seventeen-year-olds can kill who they like? Fine, I'll get all the seventeen-year-olds in Song Keng to come and stab your people if they won't have to suffer for it!"

The others saw that his eyes were red, that he was being impulsive. A smart face, but he cannot understand the law at all. Nobody knew how to explain such things as the concepts of right and wrong to this man, and nobody wanted to provoke him. "Don't provoke him, he'll calm down eventually, this can be resolved with talk."

"You're all clubbing together," he said. "Your meanings are all the same, the lives of country people are worth as much as a watermelon."

Some of the people who lived on either side of Tiexing Bridge got up to use the bathroom in the night, and those whose windows faced the river could see the watermelon boats. That night, there was also something that looked like a bundle on the shore. They knew that it wasn't a bundle, but Xiao Liang on guard.

The Song Keng people arrived to cause trouble on Toon Street after three or four days, but I can't remember it very well any more. Afterwards, everyone knew that two tractors came from Song Keng and stopped in front of the cement factory, and then about twenty people, mostly in the prime of their lives, descended from them with metal pickaxes and other such farming tools in their hands. The people at the door of the cement plant were perplexed. Then they saw Xiao Liang come flying over from Tiexing Bridge, at once wiping his tears and calling out so they could hear him clearly as he ran:

"You've arrived, it's taken you so long!"

Some of those twenty people, the ones we did not see, went directly from the cement factory to the Beida Bridge, and from there to the morgue of the Fifth People's Hospital. The others followed Xiao Liang aggressively down Toon Street to arrive at the door of Chen Suzhen's house.

Other than some rebel fighting in the northern part of the city many years ago, the residents of Toon Street had never seen such a heroic and chaotic scene as the Song Keng military delegation to Chen Suzhen's house. About twenty Song Keng people stood in front of Chen Suzhen's house, all of them trying to rush in. On account of the width of the crowd and the narrowness of the door, the door was pulled out of its frame. Those brandishing it declared that they were going to use it to carry Shoulai to keep Fu San company at the morgue. Only a few among the Song Keng people were properly dressed, most of them looking like they had only just emerged from the earth with mean faces and bodies smelling faintly of fields and dirt. Some of them had forgotten to roll their trousers back down over their knees, exposing calves caked with mud. But there was one who looked like he might be a countryside party cadre; he had no farming tools, and a fountain pen in his pocket.

Shoulai's father, Mr Liu, had only just returned from some munitions factory in Jiangxi when the Song Keng crowd burst into his home. He was in the kitchen boiling up medicine for his wife, who had been bedridden for days. She is one of those people who is always getting migraines even if nothing has happened to cause them, never mind something like this happening in her own family. As she waited for her medicine, Chen Suzhen heard the thundering of footfalls coming from outside, and then the crash as the medicine pot toppled to the ground. Her husband's loud demands of what all these people were doing in his house were muffled by the undulating rhythms of the Song Keng people's unified wrath:

"Bring him out, hand him over!"

The sound of a woman's shrill cries was intermingled with the shouting. Realising what was going on, Chen Suzhen tried to sit up from her bed but found that she could not move, her head began to swim. Run, she tried to call out, run to the police! Her voice sank beneath the bedlam. She heard the sound of the doors and windows shaking, smashing, the bowls in the cupboards rolling to the floor. She heard the sound of her husband's voice becoming lower, turning into shrieks of pain. She seized the alarm clock from her bedside and hurled it against the door.

"Don't fight them, go to the police!"

She doesn't know whether or not her husband heard the alarm clock bashing against the door, all she remembers is that a few of the invaders came rushing into her room, one of them Xiao Liang, who she recognised, and another she had never seen before, but from his slim and dark appearance she could guess straightaway that it was Fu San's brother. Chen Suzhen was not afraid. She watched them calmly as she lay there, then pronounced one word at a time as she spoke: "My son has been arrested." She thought that they must not have been listening. They said:

"Bring him out, bring him out!"

"It's no use you coming here," said Chen Suzhen. "A life for a life, it's the law, he will be executed. They said:

"Bring him out, bring him out!" Realising that her words were of no use, she fell silent as she lay there quietly gazing at the pickaxes in their hands.

"If you think that one life is not enough," she said, "then take mine as well, I'm not afraid."

She watched those pickaxes in their hands, and she believed that they wouldn't dare. Her eyes rose bravely to meet the frustrated stare of Fu San's brother. He looked away first. Averting his face, Fu San's brother's expression rested on her pillow, on a piece of biscuit that her husband had been eating earlier.

"You're eating biscuits?" He certainly was Fu San's brother. He lifted the colourful sheet beneath Chen Suzhen's body and saw the straw mat beneath it. "You put a sheet on the straw mat on your bed," he said. "You sleep so comfortably?" He lifted the pickaxe in his hand to hit the coffee-coloured lacquer of the bedstead as his tone of ridicule turned to anger.

"You sleep on such a bed and you've raised such a filthy animal?" A fire burned in the depths of his eyes. "It was you who raised him wasn't it? Three days and three nights my Ma has cried, and she hasn't touched a drop of water. And here you are, sleeping, lying here, eating biscuits!"

Then, either because they could not bear the sight of her lying there or because they could not bear the sight of the biscuit by her side, the Song Keng people did something that Chen Suzhen would never forget. It was Fu San's brother who began it all, snatching up the biscuit and throwing it to the ground where he trampled it to pieces.

"Smash up her bed," he called to the others, "then let's see her lie here eating biscuits!" Chen Suzhen's body jolted up and down on the bed as they hit its frame with their pick-axes. She never could have expected this type of bizarre humiliation, and she had no strength at all to prevent it. She began to cry as her body was bouncing, to'ing and fro'ing hilariously on the straw mat such that her nerve collapsed along with the bed frame. Suddenly, she felt that she was sinking; the bed had collapsed on one side to create a steep slope from which her body promptly rolled, like a delivery of concrete to the wharf.

That day, Mr Liu knew that the tools in the Song Keng people's hands were aimed not at himself and his wife, but at his furniture. He knew that they intended in this way to take reprisals but, in his panic and inability to bear this savage punishment, he picked up a vegetable knife. The result was that all the Song Keng people were reminded of the watermelon knife and one of them cried:

"The child learned from the father, they're all killers!"

How could they know that Mr Liu was a man with a

good reputation, not at all like his son. But, on that day and regardless of right or wrong, they gathered around him to teach him a lesson. It is unknown whose tool actually did it, but once Mr Liu had ended up down on the rice vat he could not get back up again. Later, we learnt that three of his ribs had been broken.

The person who went to report the incident was their neighbour, Aunty Qian. Aunty Qian had been trying to enter Chen Suzhen's house, all the while saying that it was fine that they had come to settle their dispute as long as they did not carry on about it so loudly – there are neighbours here on the night shift, how are they to get their rest with you turning heaven and earth upside down – when she discovered both that the Song Keng people had set up guards to block her, and that they would not listen to her. She went away in a huff, saying:

"This isn't your territory, if you won't listen to me then just wait and see who comes next!"

At first two of the local police came, an old and a young one, each relying on their uniforms to gain entrance to Chen Suzhen's home. The older of the pair was Comrade Qin, a well-known man on Toon Street with a lot of experience; as soon as he entered the house he knew that the situation was going to be difficult to control. While Comrade Qin assessed Mr Liu's wounds and tried to persuade the Song Keng people to leave, his younger colleague thoughtlessly brought out his handcuffs and snapped them onto somebody's wrist – the result being that he found himself quite suddenly at the centre of a circle made by the points of around twenty farming tools. Pulling him to the side, Comrade Qin said something into the youth's ear which caused him to squeeze out from the heap of people. Where was he going? To get backup.

After that a truck arrived from the Dongfeng chemical plant. Only about seven or eight people came rushing out of it, all wearing military belts over their blue workers' uniforms and carrying rifles. That was the first time that the people around Chen Suzhen's house had ever seen a rifle so close up, and so there was one boy who shouted out in his high voice:

"They're the workers' militia, their rifles are fakes!

"Fake," demanded the annoyed militiamen, "want me to try shooting you with it then?"

Silence fell over Chen Suzhen's house the moment the rifles entered. First the militia dragged out the Song Keng people's tools, throwing them into the truck. The crowd counted as they came; one, two, three, four... seven or eight pickaxes and five or six rakes, even two sickles. After the tools came the people, pulled out one by one. The crowd counted those too; one, two, three, four, all together seventeen or eighteen people, two of them women, and one of the pair lactating. I did not know then what her relationship was to Fu San, but her voice was abnormally sharp. She used her hand to wipe milk from the front of her jacket as she cried and shouted to the crowd. I did not hear what she was actually saying, but the look in her eyes as she faced the crowd made it seem that she wanted our help, wanted us to criticise the militia's behaviour.

The men were all put into the truck to be taken off to wherever the matter could be investigated further, but the two women were allowed to stay. At the beginning the two of them just stood there, one of them continuously wiping at her tears and the other lactating away while she talked nonstop to the assembled crowd. It is hard to understand a Song Keng accent when they talk so quickly, but we could hear by then that she was indeed trying to win sympathy.

"A good man comes to sell watermelons, and you think his life is as cheap as his wares? He's dead, and we cannot even come to settle the matter?"

It was inappropriate for the listeners to tell her their own positions. Someone, curious to know what her relationship with the dead man was, could not help themselves but ask:

"You two women, which of you is Fu San's wife?" The lactating woman shook her head. "I'm his little sister."

"The other?" The other did not speak, but the lactating woman introduced her:

"She's his sister too, Fu San's little sister."

Fu San's sisters had not been asked to get on the truck, and I don't know why but when they heard it start, they shrieked and leapt up to grab it, one on the left and one on the right, each of them pulling back on the tailgate in refusal to let it leave. But their strength was not enough, and so the breastfeeding woman ran to lie down at its front wheel.

I still do not know her name, but as Fu San's sister lay there on the ground she looked death in the face like some-body we had only ever seen in movies. That is what made the deepest impression on us, but no matter how you look at it we could not have seen her - with her wet chest and disordered clothes exposing her bulging stomach - as a heroine. Many people ran to the front of the truck to get a look at her, more and more crowding onto Toon Street until that narrow road became blocked. After the traffic jam began, children started to blow whistles all over the place, their collective din making the air boil with excitement.

The fact that the director of the northern city police department, Lao Jin, came to deal with the situation personally is enough to show how thorny the matter really was. According to the people of Toon Street, Lao Jin had the ability to solve any dispute with ease – but without the proper documents, and when this storm between worker and peasant relations had already deteriorated to such an extent, he really had no means of disentangling the mess. His expression turned sour. At that point, Lao Jin found the Song Keng man who looked like a party cadre and asked him to persuade Fu San's sister to move. With a sly twinkle in his eye, the cadre said:

"She doesn't want to live, run her over. Our lives aren't worth anything to you anyway."

It seemed that even this cadre did not understand the concept of the law, and so could not help to uphold it. Getting angry himself, Lao Jin rolled up his sleeves and declared that the situation was like refusing to drink a toast only to be forced to drink a forfeit.

"Come on," he said, "lift her onto the vehicle!"

It was in such a straightforward way that the problem was solved. We watched as Fu San's little sister was lifted onto the truck by several people. She fought, but her struggles were useless against them, they lifted her up lightly as her fearful cries intermingled with strings of Song Keng curses. As she struggled, somebody worked their way through the crowd and, pushing their head out from deep between the shoulders of the other people, chirruped the line:

"Just like a dying pig. This country woman is fierce!"

By then everybody there knew the ins and outs of the story. Sentiments would blow east, then suddenly west, and then all at once everybody was inclined towards the side of the Song Keng people. It is impossible to explain this position in a few words. All one can say is that he who makes no investigation into a situation has no right to make a judgement of it.

All that chaos went on for a long time, but the truck eventually got going with the Song Keng people on board; men and women together, an exhausted expression overcoming every face. To look at them, it seemed that some of them had become frightened or deterred, their fearful and confused expressions quite pitiful. Some, including Xiao Liang, knew many of the assembled crowd from when they had come to buy watermelons and so just looked a bit sheepish. Yet there were some who still retained their wrathful expressions, Fu San's brother, for example, who still glared at either side of the street. But the most fearless of them was that party cadre. He stood on the truck playing with the fountain pen in his pocket, his face intentionally arrogant but still with the posture of a leader. He waved his hand here and there, but those on the street found nobody when they looked left and right to see who it was that he was waving to. They guessed that his intention was to show that he was not afraid, but many realised that the casual gesture was just like Mao Zedong's when he received the Red Guards at Tiananmen.

One day in early September, Fu San's mother arrived.

At first nobody knew who she was - there was just an old woman walking around on Tiexing Bridge wearing a blue jacket, black trousers and straw sandals. A towel on her head marked her out as dressing in the typical style of an old woman from Song Keng. That Song Keng woman stood on the bridge gazing at both sides of the river, rubbing her eyes as she looked around. It was obvious that she had cataracts, and perhaps they had blocked her vision so much so that she could see nothing at all from up there. She came down to the end of the bridge and held her hand to her forehead to scan the water, but she still did not see what she was looking for. It was Shen Lan, the local kindergarten teacher, who was walking past the old woman, when she asked:

"Sister, where has the watermelon boat gone that was here in the summer?"

But Shen Lan is an outlander who only speaks standard Mandarin with the children, she could not understand what this Song Keng dialect meant.

"Go to the Neighbourhood Committee," she replied. The old woman had no reaction, as if she did not know what a Neighbourhood Committee was. Using her finger to point to a red lacquered window on the other side of the river, Shen Lan said: "A Neighbourhood Committee is a Neighbourhood Committee. You cross the bridge, go over there, and inside is the Neighbourhood Committee."

But Fu San's mother's eyes were no good, she could neither see the red lacquered window on the other side of the river nor understand the meaning of Neighbourhood Committee.

"Sister," she said, "I'm looking for a watermelon boat, a boat!

Sensing the other woman's impatience, her face split into an appeasing smile. A watermelon boat, that boat that caused a life to be lost. Now Shen Lan could guess who this Song Keng woman really was. She watched as Fu San's mother gurgled in her throat, making a sound as if she were about to cry and lifting her hand to apply pressure to her neck. She soothed it, soothed it down, and finally she really managed to suppress the sob. Shen Lan was surprised to see the old woman's smile return.

"Sister," she said, "help me. My eyes are no good, I can't see."

The watermelon boat was not there. Shen Lan went down to the stone dock and searched the river. She saw little boats selling garlic or fish, an iron boat dredging up river mud, a barge transporting concrete and even a stinking cesspit boat which stopped at the public toilets – but there was no trace of the watermelon boat.

"How is it not here?" she said. "I walk past here every day and I see it right here. There were strong winds yesterday, I bet it was blown away, and if it was blown away then it cannot have been blown far."

"Sister," said Fu San's mother, "would it have blown to the east or to the west? Tell me, I've cried so much that I won't be able to see."

"I can't see it either," said Shen Lan. "Let me take you to the Neighborhood Committee, they'll help you find it."

And so, Shen Lan led Fu San's mother across the Tiexing Bridge. As they reached the top, Shen Lan turned to her and asked:

"You're this old, and your eyes are no good. Why is it that you have come to find the boat yourself?"

"It isn't our family's boat, Fu San borrowed it from Wang Lin. Fu San isn't here any more, so I need to take it back to Wang Lin."

"That's not what I meant, I meant to ask; you're so old, how are you going to scull the boat all the way back to Song Keng?"

"Slowly. I'll scull it slowly and I'll scull it for two days and then I'll be home."

She had still misunderstood Shen Lan's meaning and so she asked straightforwardly:

"Is there nobody in your family with strength? I heard that Fu San's brother and sisters all got locked up? Have they not been released?"

Fu San's mother hesitated this time before getting closer to Shen Lan and saying into her ear:

"You're a good person, sister, and so I'm not afraid to tell you. Fu San's brother and sisters were released yesterday."

"In that case you should get them to come and pick up the boat."

Fu San's mother looked at the bridge, then the space underneath it, then softly she said:

"I don't dare. I don't dare say anything, either. The police said that they would take pity on us this time, and they won't make us pay for the family's losses or their medical expenses. But they said that if we come back and if we break the law again, then we'll be in real trouble."

Fu San's mother was led to the Neighborhood Committee leader, Director Cui. Director Cui was occupied with preparing posters for the Patriotic Health Month, but despite all that she went to fetch Fu San's mother a glass of water and told her not to worry.

"It's such a big boat, no matter where the wind took it, it's still on the water somewhere; it can't have sprouted wings and flown off. It will have gone to the Beida Bridge, and if it has gone any further than that," she said, "we'll still be able to solve the matter with the director of the Taohuating Neighbourhood Committee.

Shen Lan's directions to the Neighbourhood Committee proved to be a critical step in the search for the watermelon boat. Even though the Neighbourhood Committee relies on the public, which is a messy business, there will always be those who will report incidents – particularly in the case of such a large boat. Two days ago, somebody had reported to Director Cui that a young man called Crooked Mouth had taken advantage of the unguarded boat, boarded it, and carried away the remaining watermelons in his own large bamboo basket. Over the course of the two days since, the whole of Toon Street's cadre population was either solving Chen Suzhen's family problem or preparing for Patriotic Health Month; nobody found time to investigate the removal of a few watermelons and the matter had been pushed aside.

Director Cui sent for Crooked Mouth. She did not disclose the identity of the old woman in the room when she asked him to confess how many watermelons he had taken. The man looked at Director Cui from the corner of his eye and, guessing that she already knew the answer to her own question, responded to it with another.

"How many did you say were left?"

"How many you say, that's how many there were." Adopting a stern tone, Director Cui said: "Am I asking you or are you asking me? I'm telling you, Crooked Mouth, you go around pilfering things and you think we cadres are none the wiser. It's all written in the books; you've just got cocky because we haven't come to find you for a few days!"

At that, Crooked Mouth began to speak frankly, saying: "There aren't many left and they're going to rot whether I take them or not. Some of them are rotten already."

"How many? Tell me, if you do, that'll be the end of it. If you don't then you'll be telling the police."

"Eleven or twelve, but they're mostly rotten."

"OK, then we'll cut it in half. Six melons. One melon is worth three *mao*, so you owe one *quai* eight *mao*."

It was then that Crooked Mouth began to pay attention to the old woman on the bench. He saw the towel on her head, and he knew that she was from Song Keng. Suddenly raising his voice to roar at her, he said:

"For that many rotten melons – it's daylight robbery!"

Fu San's mother stood up in fright.

"Brother, what are you saying, I've never robbed anybody. Those who rob get what's coming to them. I'm looking for a boat, brother, did you take the boat?"

"I just took melons. Do I look like Heavenly King Li? How could I carry off a boat? Don't ask me where your son's boat is, ask Wang Deji's son. I saw him playing on it with another kid, they were sculling it under Tiexing Bridge."

To atone for his misdeeds, Director Cui sent Crooked Mouth to go and fetch Wang Deji's son, Anping.

"If I go and get him," said Crooked Mouth as he leaned on the doorway, "I won't be in trouble?"

"I haven't decided yet," replied the director. "They aren't my melons. You ask this old lady."

Crooked Mouth turned his head to face Fu San's mother.

"Do you or do you not want me to pay you? If you do, I'll give you five *mao*."

Fu San's mother waved her hands. "No, no, no, I'm not here to collect melon money. I'm here to take back my son's boat. Please help me, brother. Help me find the boat."

Fu San's mother wanted to go with Crooked Mouth, but both he and Director Cui objected and so she sat there by the window, looking at the river outside. Director Cui gave her another glass of water which she politely declined, saying that she would not be able to drink it. Then, she asked Director Cui if that old woman who sold spring onions under Tiexing Bridge was still there, saying that she was a good person who had offered her water, too.

"Which old woman? Do you know her surname?" She didn't know. She could only say that she had a mole on the corner of her mouth. But Director Cui had her own responsibilities and hummed to herself as she carried on with them, not really wanting to stay and chat with Fu San's mother. Nonetheless, she heard the old woman say:

"When I was young I used to scull to Tiexing Bridge to sell cabbage. I knew a lot of people back then."

Director Cui didn't look up as she replied: "Who did you know?"

Pausing to think for a moment, Fu San's mother said: "The person who works at the boiled water store, the person at the herbal medicine store, and the person at the tobacco shop. I know all those people."

"The boiled water store has been demolished," said Director Cui, "and the herbal medicine shop has been modernised."

Fu San's mother sighed. "Later on I had five younger

sisters to look after, I had no time to come to Tiexing Bridge with the cabbages. It's been twenty years. They wouldn't be able to recognise me, and I've cried so much I couldn't recognise them either."

At that moment, Crooked Mouth entered with Anping. Once he had done so, his mission was complete, and he washed his hands of the affair. Standing calm and composed at the door and picking his nose, Anping looked from one woman to the other.

"Wang Anping," said Director Cui, "what did you do with the boat?"

"I don't know," replied Anping. "Where did it go?"

"Wasn't it you who sculled it?" asked Director Cui. "You don't know who did?"

"All I did was untie it," said Anping. "Who said I was sculling it? It was Dasheng who was sculling it. We moved it to the opening of the bridge and it just moved off by itself, got stuck in the bridge opening. We just got on it."

Copying his tone, Director Cui repeated: "You just got on it? You scull somebody else's boat, get it stuck in the bridge and you think that's fine?"

"But the boat isn't stuck, it's floated off," said Anping.

Director Cui became angry and said: "It floated off, and you think that isn't your responsibility? Go and get Dasheng. I'm making you responsible for recovering that boat and if you don't, well, we'll see what Wang Deji has to say about it."

Fu San's mother could not sit still on her stool. She stood up and pulled on Director Cui's clothes, saying:

"That was a good talk with the child, Comrade Cui."

With that, she went up to him and lowered herself to his

height, patting at his trousers and forcing a smile to cover her heavy expression.

"Good brother," she said, "we country folk cannot live without boats."

"Why are you patting my trousers," said Anping. "They're not dusty!"

He looked at her with disgust as she patted them again.

"Good brother," she said, trying to pat his head, but the boy was having none of it. He dodged backwards, leaving Fu San's mother's hand hanging in the air. He continued about his nose picking and tilted his eyes at her before suddenly saying:

"Is it your son that Shoulai stabbed?"

Director Cui leapt up and hit the boy's head with her newspaper, saying:

"If I don't go and tell Wang Deji then my name isn't Cui!"

She turned back to Fu San's mother who just stood there, bent at the waist and trembling a little as usual. The old woman waved her hand.

"It's just child's talk, I'm not upset." She lifted the corner of her jacket and wiped her eyes. "It's my fate. It's no use getting upset with other people about it. The year before last my old man died, last year I lost three of my sows to fever, and this year it's Fu San. One disaster a year, my tears are all dried up. When I cry, I cry so hard that I give myself these headaches, and when they come I have no strength. I need to scull that boat back home, so I can't cry."

Bring that boat back. Director Cui could tell that this matter was greater than all heaven as far as Fu San's mother was concerned, but the old woman's state of mind relieved the cadre. She sighed with relief, for there were some women who felt that the Neighbourhood Committee was the ideal place for wailing and fainting, none of which Director Cui could abide. But Fu San's mother neither cried nor shouted, arousing sympathy along with a feeling of good fortune in the director's heart. The only thorn was that boat – she didn't know where it had blown to, she didn't even know whether it was still within her jurisdiction or beyond the Beida Bridge. Unable to give up her work to find it herself, she turned solemnly to the little boy.

"Schoolboy Wang Anping, listen to me. Go and take this old lady to find her boat. Take her from Tiexing Bridge all the way up to Beida Bridge. I'm holding you responsibile for this task, and if you don't do it I have one other option. What option? You don't know? Whether you really don't know or you're just pretending, it's simple. I'll go and get Wang Deji to fulfil your responsibility for you!"

That afternoon, we all saw Wang Deji's son taking Fu San's mother along the riverbank. Some of the onlookers pointed to the old woman and asked him:

Is that your grandma? Your grandma's from Song Keng?"

"It's your grandma!" Anping shouted back unhappily. "Your grandma's from Song Keng!"

Taking no notice of the discrimination against Song Keng, the old woman smiled hospitably to passersby as she asked:

"Comrade, have you seen a Song Keng watermelon boat?"

"Do you want me to find it for you or not?" said Anping. If you want me to find it then don't go around asking everyone else. And you're not speaking clearly, it's 'boat' not 'bar'. They think you're looking for liquor!"

Fu San's mother tried once again to ruffle the boy's hair, stretching out her hand and then pulling it back, saying:

"Good brother. Grandma's eyes are broken, I cannot see, I need your help."

Anping snorted.

"Do you know what the phrase '*be like Lei Feng*' means? It means act like the heroic soldier Lei Feng, and Director Cui is forcing me to do it. She'll get my dad to come and deal with me if I don't, the old witch!"

When they arrived at Dasheng's house, Anping told Fu San's mother to wait there while he went inside to see. Opening the unlocked door, Anping rushed straight inside shouting Dasheng's name. He rushed through without a care, dashing through the room and to the window overlooking the river. Li Jinzhi, Dasheng's mother, had been at her sewing machine working on a curtain seam when she leapt with fright.

"Damn it, child, what are you doing? You'll scare me to death!"

"I'm looking for Dasheng!" said Anping.

"He's not here!" said Li Jinzhi. "Didn't his father warn you not to come calling for him any more? You lead him into trouble."

Anping laughed coldly.

"Warn me? Who thinks calling for him is all that special, anyway? I'm telling you, I'm being like Lei Feng right now, I'm finding a boat."

By this time Anping had already climbed onto Dasheng's bed and, kneeling, was opening the window to check out who was by the river outside. Li Jinzhi got up and started to hit him with her fabric ruler.

"Don't hit me!" shouted Anping. "I'm being like Lei Feng! It's a boat, did you see it passing the window?"

Using all her effort to drag the boy from the bed, she reluctantly listened to the boy's explanation.

"What boat?" she said. "I haven't seen a boat. I'm not lying, I sit there every day and I've seen no boat."

Anping suddenly shouted: "It's the boat that belongs to the man Shoulai killed! Li Jinzhi jumped with fright again before becoming indignant, beating Anping about the shoulders with her ruler as she shouted:

"Beast of a child, damn it, what are you doing coming to my house searching for a dead man's boat, why not go to your own! Stirring up all this bad luck, watch out I don't go and find Wang Deji, he'll beat you to death!"

Avoiding her ruler, Anping leapt from Dasheng's bed, still explaining himself as he moved. "My house isn't on the river, how am I going to find a boat there? Stupid woman!"

At that, Anping ran outside with Li Jinzhi in such swift pursuit that she nearly bumped into Fu San's mother.

"Sister," said Fu San's mother to Li Jinzhi. This would have been unusual, seeing as the old woman was so much Li Jinzhi's senior, but she knew that this was a Song Keng habit and so, suddenly realising that the boy was not lying, she let go of Anping.

"It was your son..." but she only asked half of the question, swallowing the rest as she realised what she was about to say. Li Jinzhi worked at the same textile mill as Shoulai's mother Chen Suzhen, and they didn't get along. As a result, Li Jinzhi could not help herself but say:

"That boy Shoulai, I mean it, I've known since he was small that he would bring disaster. His parents totally spoiled him!"

Not receiving any answer from Fu San's mother, Li Jinzhi realised her error; that was nonsense, she might not know who had killed him yet. Fu San's mother looked confused and began to follow Anping away, but Li Jinzhi pulled her back.

"Come in, have some water!"

"Thank you so much, sister, but I've drunk enough water, I can't have any more. Sister, you live by the river, you haven't seen the boat?"

Without even thinking, Li Jinzhi said that she had not. Then, suddenly recalling the image of the fool Guangchun carrying a sculling pole as he passed by her bike, her eyes lit up and she shouted after them:

"Wait, wait, I'll take you to the fool Guangchun."

It was in this way that Fu San's mother was turned back the way she had come, to the fool Guangchun's house.

At Guangchun's house, Li Jinzhi came up against the obstacle of Guangchun's grandmother.

"He might be a fool," said the woman, "but he has never stolen anything. After she had said this, she asked when it was that Li Jinzhi saw him taking people's things.

"He hasn't taken people's things," said Li Jinzhi. "He's taken somebody's scull!" Li Jinzhi pointed at Fu San's mother. "Look at her, look!"

Peeping outside, Guangchun's grandmother saw only an old woman from Song Keng standing bent-waisted at a lamppost.

"Who's that?"

Li Jinzhi lowered her voice.

"That's the watermelon boatman Fu San's mother. Guangchun doesn't understand anything," she said. "You're the one who burns the incense, who chants to the Buddha. How can you have that sculling pole in your house?"

Grandma Shaoxing's expression coloured. She lifted her bound feet and rushed into the inner courtyard of her house, shouting as she went.

"Guangchun, Guangchun, you say you're not a fool but if you're not a fool then how have you brought something like that into this house!"

As Li Jinzhi followed, she immediately saw the fool Guangchun in the courtyard, guarding the scull. The scull was worn, its tung oil all shabby to reveal the dark wood beneath. So long in contact with the water, now it was removed it looked like just the sort of old weapon which might suit the boy's imagined military career. Guangchun's grandma had left some pickled vegetables drying out on top of it, and a mop still dripping with water was resting at its side. Li Jinzhi, not caring about the particulars of the matter, brought the scull out of the door and shouted over to Fu San's mother:

"Is this yours?"

Fu San's mother came over, blinking those eyes that could not see. As she touched it, she said: "It is, it's our scull! I've been using that scull for twenty years, I know it. It used to have a handle of red cloth."

Sighing, Li Jinzhi said that the scull must have been on the boat, so we can see whether or not the fool remembers where it was. She was just about to enter the house when the fool Guangchun was pushed out of the door by his grandmother, holding a military salute to Fu San's mother as he came. The old woman followed him out and shook the other's hand, saying:

"My boy's brain is not too good, he just wanted to play at having a weapon. Don't quarrel with him, he told me he found it abandoned at the brewery wharf!"

As dusk fell on that day, we all saw a crowd of people making their way towards the brewery wharf, a scull shared between their shoulders. The fool Guangchun strode proudly at the front of his motley military cohort; Wang Deji's son, Li Jinzhi, Grandma Shaoxing and an old woman with a towel on her head. It was then that we all knew, the woman whose hand Grandma Shaoxing was holding was Fu San's mother. More and more people joined them as they walked. Anping was not tall enough to carry the scull and so wanted to run around, but at that moment Wang Deji came home from work, and he dared not run away. His father, seeing his child out of the house, came over with his bike as he roared:

"Get back inside!"

Anping jumped back to stand behind Fu San's mother. Pointing at her, he said: "I'm like Lei Feng! If you don't believe me then ask her!"

After all this had happened, Wang Deji would say that he found the sight of Fu San's mother shocking; never in his life had he seen a mother who so closely resembled her son. However, the shock lay not in the similarity between their faces, but the fact that as the woman stood there, bent at the waist with exhaustion and with one hand reaching out to shake his, the gesture seemed to him to be the mirror image of Fu San's silhouette as he leant against the wall of the lavatory, reaching out to hand him the watermelon knife.

It had only been left for twenty days, but already nobody would have recognised that watermelon boat from Song Keng. It had been squeezed into a corner among all the brewery boats and emitting that desolate smell particular to abandoned boats. The wheat straw on the canopy had all vanished, and of the four supporting poles only one remained, standing solitary like a crude flagpole in a schoolyard. The oven was gone, too, certainly on account of human intervention as it had been destroyed so utterly and neatly that not even half a brick remained. It is unknown who had been on the boat other than the fool Guangchun, but somebody had left cinders on it, and it was covered with water and leaves. The cabin was so filthy that it looked like one of those boats that collects trash in the summertime.

Li Jinzhi stood on the wharf and pointed to the liquor delivery boats, raising her voice to criticise those on board.

"How can you all be so rotten? Your boats are all clean but you let this happen. Clean it up, how can you turn somebody's boat into a trash barge?"

The brewery boat people called back: "You insult us and then you ask for a favour? If we hadn't brought it here it would be in the Pacific Ocean by now!"

"Big sister," said Fu San's mother to comfort Li Jinzhi, "you don't need to quarrel. If the boat's here then all is well."

With that, the old woman's eyes moved over to Wang Deji and the others holding her scull and, marvelling as she did at their clumsiness on the water, moved to board the boat. Li Jinzhi was just about to help her when she realised that the old woman was already on board.

It was a typical September dusk, the river water sparkled as sunlight the colour of yellow rice wine hit the brewery wharf, fragrant and flowing. It was the fool Guangchun who first pointed out the bloodstain on the prow of the boat.

"Look at that bloodstain," he said to Anping. "Don't you think it looks like an ox?"

Their eyes, which had all been watching Fu San's mother and Wang Deji holding the scull, were now drawn to follow Guangchun's finger. Sure enough, there was something that, while not quite like an ox, was still very clearly blood. Everybody stared at the coffee-coloured stain. Li Jinzhi's eyes widened and she pressed her finger to her lips, signalling to everyone not to say a word.

"Her eyes aren't good, she said, it would be best that she just didn't know."

Anping didn't hear her.

"Bloodstains are really hard to clean," he said, "showing off his knowledge of such matters to the fool Guangchun. Water won't cut it. You need to rub it with ethanol. Go and get some ethanol, then we can try it right now."

"Where can I get ethanol from?" asked the fool Guangchun. Anping was stumped. Rolling his eyes, he said:

"Forget it. It would be a waste of time to show you, anyway. All you know is whether it looks like an ox or a horse!"

Afterwards, when the only person left on the boat was Fu San's mother, the brewery boats had already been moved to create a passageway through the water for the old woman. Nobody in the crowd at Wang Deji's side could handle boats, and so they could only watch from the shore as she slowly sculled away.

"Did you see the bloodstain?" Li Jinzhi turned to ask.

"How could I not?" answered Wang Deji. "I just didn't dare make a sound."

Li Jinzhi sighed.

"Her eyes are no good. It's better for her that she doesn't see it. She'd lose the strength to scull the boat if she saw her own son's blood."

"Song Keng is dozens of *li* away from here by water," said Wang Deji. "Her family can't know that she has come all this way to scull the boat. They never would have let her if they did!"

As she sculled the boat away, the swaying motion of Fu San's mother's body suddenly stopped. Slowly turning around, the old woman lifted her elbow to rub at her eyes, straining herself to look back towards Li Jinzhi and the others standing there on the wharf. It looked like she wanted to say goodbye. She wanted to say goodbye to those people on the dock, but they were too far from her blurred eyes and she could not distinguish between the silhouettes of those well-meaning Toon Street people and the piles of liquor jugs from the brewery. She fell to her knees and lowered her head towards the jugs. The fool Guangchun began to laugh.

"Why is she kowtowing to those jars of yellow liquor?"

But the adults were not fools. They knew that Fu San's mother could not see, that she was facing the wrong direction. Waving their arms, they called out to her.

"Please, get up, we don't deserve such an honour!"

She got up, a tiny figure in the distance thrown into dark and incoherent shadow by the sunset. It was in this way, on a September dusk, that the last watermelon boat left the brewery wharf. According to the estimation of Wang Deji, who goes there to fix tractors, it is about sixty *li* to Song Keng by water, so she will certainly have had to spend a night on the boat. After all, she was quite old and did not look like she was sculling the boat as smoothly as the other people from Song Keng could. Perhaps she was tired. Her sculling was slow, and so was the boat. In fact, it looked like it was not her sculling the boat at all, but rather the boat leading her to the lower reaches of the river. Toward the lower reaches of the river, that was the way to Song Keng. No matter how bad her eyesight was, Fu San's mother would always remember the way to Song Keng.

Wang Deji stood with the others at the top of the wharf, watching that symbol of summertime float away. They come, and they go. According to the solar calendar, there are actually two seasons that separate summer from autumn.

IV

Pretty As Angels

像天使一样美丽

THE GIRLS ON OUR STREET are like the boys, from small to big they form together into natural groups, three to five in each, with no communication whatsoever between them, and if they ever should meet in the narrow street they twitter in their companions' ears, sometimes even spitting in the direction of the other gang. It's a Toon Street custom, and I did say it had plenty of odd ones.

Xiaoyuan and Zhuzhu formed a group of two very early on. Xiaoyuan's house stood beside the chemical plant, while Zhuzhu's was at the very bottom of the mulberry garden, separated from each other both by the lengthy Toon Street and the stone bridge which spanned the river. Nevertheless, the two were inseparable. Every day, Zhuzhu would arrive at Xiaoyuan's house in the early morning, from where they would either walk to school together or hang out in the street when they were off school. Xiaoyuan has always been slim and tall, promising to become sweet-tempered and pretty when she matures. Zhuzhu meanwhile was short and a little plump, but with a pair of beautiful black grape eyes. The former was accustomed to wearing T-strapped shoes and an old, men's-style military uniform, while the latter's was new and a little small, although still of the same military style. They would carry cloth bags over their shoulders as they walked down long Toon Street, inevitably passing by the herbal medicine shop on their way. At its doorway there always lingered a man whom everybody called Crazy Lu, standing there clutching a bunch of Chinese medicine in his hand. It was he who gave the girls reason to quicken their pace as they passed, for when he saw them, he would often say the same sentence; you two are as pretty as angels.

"You two are as pretty as angels," said Crazy Lu.

. . .

It was difficult for the boys to grasp the intangible and ever changing geopolitics of the girls' associations with any certainty. Later, when those of the boys who secretly admired one or the other heard the pair had split, they were quite surprised. The cause of it all was an unexpected rain-storm one afternoon. The gurgling sound of the rain made the middle school students anxious in their classroom. When class was over, most of the boys dashed out into the torrent using their book bags as cover, while the girls stayed behind chatting in the corridors as they waited for their families to fetch them their rain gear. On that day, Xiaoyuan and Zhuzhu were as close as ever. Zhuzhu was loudly and merrily chastising the history teacher for picking his nose while teaching, but Xiaoyuan's expression showed that there was something on her mind and, as she watched the rain splatter onto the playground, she wondered how it was that it had not yet stopped, thinking to herself that the clothes and quilt that she had hung out to dry would already be wet through.

"He's so gross." Zhuzhu pulled on Xiaoyuan's arm, her laughter melodious and free. "Did you see him flicking his snot onto the floor? Don't you think he's so gross?"

"This damned rain, when will it end!"

Xiaoyuan pushed away Zhuzhu's hand impatiently and said:

"I'm so worried, my mum's at work and my sweater and my quilt are outside getting soaked!"

Then Miao Qing suddenly called out Xiaoyuan's name. These girls were not conversant, there had never been a word shared between them before and yet here she stood, lingering in the rain with her cotton-print umbrella, turning her head to look at Xiaoyuan and Zhuzhu. She had an arrogant and conspiratorial look in her eyes as she stepped in front of Xiaoyuan.

"Come on Xiaoyuan," said Miao Qing, "we can go together."

Dumbfounded, Xiaoyuan looked to Zhuzhu who didn't hesitate to show her distaste by hurling a ball of spit down the corridor.

"You go, I'm waiting here" whispered Xiaoyuan softly. Miao Qing rotated the handle of the umbrella in her palm, a sneer appearing at the corners of her mouth.

"You're like a dog snapping at the heels of one of the eight immortals," she said. "You can't tell a good person when you see one." Xiaoyuan looked at Zhuzhu again who cursed at Miao Qing.

"You need to clean your mouth out, who's the dog here! You're the dog, wagging your tail every time you see someone." Zhuzhu held Xiaoyuan's hand, felt it slowly begin to slip away and was amazed at the embarrassed and worried expression on Xiaoyuan's face.

"I'm going," said Xiaoyuan as she turned to look at Miao Qing's back. "I need to go home and put away my clothes." Immediately, she rushed down the corridor. Zhuzhu heard her voice rise sharply in the rain.

"Miao Qing, wait for me, I'm coming."

Zhuzhu was left alone, watching their figures huddled together under the umbrella as they disappeared into the rain. Her stupefied tears would not stop flowing; the greatest love of her girlhood had received its deepest blow. She dried the tears on her face and, hitting her schoolbag against a concrete pillar, repeated a phrase over and over in her mouth: traitor, traitor, traitor.

Sunlight had returned the next day and Xiaoyuan waited anxiously for Zhuzhu, but Zhuzhu did not come. Recalling the events of the previous afternoon, she predicted there was going to be some argument between them and decided that today she simply had to walk to school alone. When she entered the gates of the Red Flag Middle School, Xiaoyuan immediately saw Zhuzhu kicking a shuttlecock with Li Qian, a game which she was particularly good at. As Zhuzhu waited for the shuttlecock to fall, she shot a glance at Xiaoyuan out of the corner of her eye.

"Traitor," said Zhuzhu.

Xiaoyuan's face turned white as snow. She hesitated a few seconds before lowering her head as she passed Zhuzhu, rummaging into her bag to feel a twist of pink ribbon which Zhuzhu had given her a few days earlier to make into a bow. Xiaoyuan took it out of her bookbag, scrunched it into a ball and threw it onto the ground. Then she went into the classroom without looking back.

From that day on, the group of two was divided. Zhuzhu had already joined Li Qian's group, and after a short period in which she preserved her solitude, Xiaoyuan sought refuge in the pretty-girl clique headed by Miao Qing.

And so, the two girls who now passed the medicine shop on Toon Street's east side on their way to school were Xiaoyuan and Miao Qing. Crazy Lu stood there grasping his medicine just as before, but somebody had shaved his head; his scalp was the same bluish grey as his lips. Xiaoyuan pulled Miao Qing past him hurriedly as the light of surprise flitted across his dull eyes. Crazy Lu's reaction was just the same as before.

"You two are as pretty as angels," said Crazy Lu.

However much Xiaoyuan wanted to know whether or not Crazy Lu said the same thing to Zhuzhu, she could not ask her; they were ignoring each other completely. When they chanced to meet at school or on the street, they would each see their own animosity mirrored on the other's face. Once, Xiaoyuan stood at a fruit stand selecting a pear when she heard that familiar sound of disdain behind her. Sensitively, she turned around and there saw Zhuzhu standing arm in arm with Li Qian. Zhuzhu stood on tiptoe and spat. Xiaoyuan could not restrain herself any more; she carefully selected a rotten pear from the crate and hurled it ferociously at Zhuzhu. She heard the other girl's scream, and that moment was one which the two former friends would never forget; as they looked into each other's faces, what they found there was shock and pain.

I have said that Xiaoyuan was a beautiful girl, and that she had also sought refuge in the clique of beauties headed by Miao Qing. Miao Qing and her gang loved taking photographs and, under their influence, Xiaoyuan naturally grew to love it too. At first, they would go together to the Worker and Peasant Photography Studio on Toon Street, but soon afterwards Miao Qing became unsatisfied with their simple equipment and their crude method of colouring the images. Thinking that the Worker and Peasant photographer always made her face look fat and ugly, Miao Qing proposed that they go instead to the Paean Photo Studio in the city centre. The photo of her mother in her wedding gown, she said, had been taken there. It was a well-respected place which could beautify your face in whatever way you wanted. The girls deferred to Miao Qing's judgment unquestioningly, and happily accepted her idea.

And so, one afternoon in May saw the four girls going to the Paean Photo Studio together. Their bags were stuffed with garments of every colour and for every season; new-style woollen sweaters and patterned skirts, winter fur coats and even a stage-costume for dressing up as a traditional Uyghur girl. They smeared glistening red lipstick over their lips and held their skirts high as they ran up and down the stairs of the photo studio. Only Xiaoyuan sat quietly to the side, insisting on not wearing any makeup.

"Try it," said Miao Qing as she slipped her rouge box to Xiaoyuan. "Put a little on and you'll be really beautiful." Xiaoyuan shook her head.

"I'm not putting it on," she said. "My mum won't let me wear rouge or lipstick and I'll be in so much trouble if she finds out."

For her first picture, a two-inch profile, Xiaoyuan wore that old, paling military uniform. For her second, another two-inch portrait, she wore the Uyghur costume. But as she sat there beneath the glaring light, neither her posture nor her expression seemed natural. The photographer asked her to smile, but she was too ill at ease. Finally, the anxious Miao Qing had a bright idea. Standing off to the side of Xiaoyuan, the other girl began to mimic their mathematics teacher's Northern Suzhou accent, after which Xiaoyuan let out a genuine smile, candidly captured by the photographer. Afterwards, Xiaoyuan removed that costume as if it were a heavy burden.

"Miao Qing," she said. "Those photos are going to be so ugly, I'm not coming back here again."

Two weeks or so later, an enlarged colour photograph of Xiaoyuan appeared in the Paean Photo Studio window where many people all saw the pretty and adorable picture. When Miao Qing told Xiaoyuan the news, she did not believe it. Miao Qing's face revealed a strange annoyance and she said:

"Don't be a hypocrite, your mouth says you don't know, but who knows what you're secretly up to?"

It was a windy evening in late spring, the air infused with the sweet fragrance of scholar-tree blossom and the people all in a hurry when Xiaoyuan made a clandestine dash to the Paean Photo Studio. She stood there, alone, gazing up into that girl's face for a long time. That girl wore a patterned silk hat on her head, and below she wore the traditional dress of a young Uyghur girl. Her clear eyes bore a hint of melancholy, her smile shy and fleeting. "That's me." Xiaoyuan's eyes filled with tears of happiness as she became aware of her own beauty for the first time, but when somebody else approached the window while gesturing to the image, she fled to the other side of the street, afraid of being recognised. The scholar trees to her side swayed gently and a lone strand of purple blossom blew away in the breeze. Xiaoyuan watched it streak through the air when the image of Crazy Lu standing by the herbal medicine store's entrance flashed into her mind. She thought that sentence he repeated: you two are as pretty as angels. She shivered, her joyful and sweet mood quickly ousted by an empty foreboding. She returned home in the warm dusk breeze, fearful, but not understanding quite what it was that had frightened her.

. . .

Practically every girl in Red Flag Middle School knew Xiaoyuan's name, knew that her photograph hung in the window of Paean Photo Studio. Afterwards, the boys saw it too. The most daring of them called out behind her back:

"He Xiaoyuan's a Xinjiang girl, Xinjiang girl, He Xiaoyuan's a Xinjiang girl." In their ignorance, the young boys made unwarranted charges against the photo: "That He Xiaoyuan, she's pretending that she's a Uyghur from Xinjiang, she's a flirtatious little hussy."

Like I say, this was at the beginning of the seventies and we didn't get much by the way of news on Toon Street back then. As a result, people felt perfectly justified in treating this affair with Xiaoyuan's photograph as an important piece of news to pass along. People all started to look sideways at the girl who lived next door to the chemical plant, and her impending adversity was caused by her fame.

"He Xiaoyuan has body odour," said one girl to another. "Everybody thinks she's so beautiful but really, she stinks."

The groups of girls, finding this astonishing discovery extremely interesting, couldn't get enough of this rumour, all of them, but especially the one which contained Zhuzhu and Li Qian, who simply could not conceal their delight. As they passed her, they would fish their handkerchiefs out and use them to cover their mouths and noses, or they would use those same handkerchiefs to fan the air with an expression of disgust. At first, Xiaoyuan was unaware that this particular method of assault was aimed particularly at her and so she responded in kind.

"She stinks," members of the other groups would say as they turned their faces and cursed. "She's polluting the air."

"It's you who stinks," she would reply without thinking. "It's you who's polluting the air." After she had finished her retort, she would look around and slowly became aware that people were staring at her armpits. She touched her armpit, there was nothing there, neither rip nor stain on her old military jacket.

"Miao Qing," Xiaoyuan asked her desk mate, what's happening? Why are the girls staring at my armpits?"

"Don't you know?" Miao Qing used her pencil sharpener to scrape red nail polish from her fingers, looking sideways at Xiaoyuan as she spoke. "They say you've got body odour."

Xiaoyuan blanched at Miao Qing, her face turning pale as paper. Her whole body trembled in her chair and the chill of apprehension turned her into a little ball. She was silent like this for so long that when she returned from the height of sorrow, the sudden sound of her hoarse-throated voice made Miao Qing jump.

"Who made up this rumour? Tell me, who made it up?" Xiaoyuan asked Miao Qing.

"I don't know, it's probably Zhuzhu that said it first," confided Miao Qing.

An ice-cold glare moved into Xiaoyuan's eyes. She stood and looked ahead at Zhuzhu who was playing dominoes at her front-row desk with Li Qian.

"I won't forgive her," said Xiaoyuan, gnashing her teeth as she made this oath, then she pulled on Miao Qing's hand and said: "Miao Qing, you know I don't stink, why aren't you standing up for me?"

Miao Qing said nothing, she just carried on using the

pencil sharpener to scrape off her red nail polish as before. Xiaoyuan seized the pencil sharpener in Miao Qing's hand and lifted her arms as she said:

"Miao Qing, smell me and say whether or not I have body odour. Miao Qing, you have to stand up for me."

Miao Qing lifted her face and looked at Xiaoyuan's armpits, wrinkling her brow. Xiaoyuan heard her careless reply:

"I can't smell anything right now but you're wearing a sweater, how is the smell supposed to get out?"

Xiaoyuan's arms remained stiffly in the air as a tear forced its way out of her eye. Afterwards, she seized her canvas bookbag and used it to cover her face, running out of the classroom. The school bell rang out shrill and clear in the corridors for the fifth lesson of the day, with boys and girls running towards every classroom in response, but Xiaoyuan dashed off to the school gate. The girl didn't notice that her things had fallen out of her bag; her book, her pencil case, her toilet paper, and a photograph had already been picked up by the wind. It was a sample photo from the Paean Photo Studio. Even though it was uncoloured, even though it was so small, it was clearly that beautiful and proud display photo which was swirling behind her back like a breeze-borne spirit in pursuit.

There is little trace of its residents to be found in the sluggish tranquility of a Toon Street spring afternoon. Melon rinds, peanut shells and trash share the sun's reflection beneath groups of house flies which whirl in the air and on that particular afternoon, Xiaoyuan dragged her bookbag along through them all at a staggering run. As she passed the herbal medicine store, she saw the dirty, skeletal figure of Crazy Lu, shaking his handful of herbs in her direction.

"You're as pretty as an angel," he said, "but you need to take more medicine, don't be afraid to take your medicine."

Xiaoyuan dodged him, sobbing as she ran, saying:

"I don't want to be beautiful, you go and be beautiful instead, why does everyone spread rumours about me?"

Xiaoyuan's counterattack was as swift as it was ferocious.

As Zhuzhu was walking to school the next day, she noticed two tall older boys standing on the stone bridge, one of them Xiaoyuan's older brother. Thinking that they were there to admire the river, she ignored them as she chewed her bubblegum and reached the top of the bridge. But then, as she neared them, the two boys sprang out and grabbed her ponytail. She tried to cry out but her mouth and nose were already covered by the boy's hand and she heard Xiaoyuan's brother say:

"If you bully Xiaoyuan again, I'm going to throw you into that river."

Zhuzhu fell to the ground, her bubblegum tumbling out of her mouth and onto her leg, dotted with bloody foam. Then she saw the tooth in the middle of it.

"My tooth," she screamed, but the two boys had already disappeared like smoke. Somebody saw her there, crying and cursing with her mouth full of blood, and went to take her hand.

"Zhuzhu, who hit you?"

"Who do you think?" she cried as she spoke. "It was He

Xiaoyuan, she's ganged up with a bunch of hooligans and got them to knock my tooth out."

Zhuzhu was a stubborn girl. Using her handkerchief to wrap the tooth, she stopped by Xiaoyuan's window on the way to school. She picked up a brick and smashed that windowpane, chanting *"body odour, body odour"* through the demolished glass.

"You stink, He Xiaoyuan, your whole family stinks."

She saw a white face flash past on the other side of the window, and she knew that it was Xiaoyuan. She knew that Xiaoyuan would not dare to retaliate.

When Zhuzhu arrived at school, she went straight to the headmaster's office, unwrapping the tooth in her handkerchief and sobbing.

"It was He Xiaoyuan. She ganged up on me with hooligans. He Xiaoyuan got two scoundrels to come and knock my tooth out."

And so, Xiaoyuan was summoned to the headmaster's office by both the headmaster and her teacher, who made her look at the tooth on the table. She ignored it, turning her head to survey the posters on the wall with an expression of peaceful apathy instead.

"Did you get someone to hit Xiao Zhuzhu?"

"It serves her right."

"Why did you want to hit her?"

"She's been spreading rumours about me."

"What rumours? You think you can hit someone for spreading rumours?"

Xiaoyuan lowered her head. She did not defend herself

while she listened to the two teachers taking it in turns to reprimand her. The headmaster said that she should write a self-criticism to understand her mistake. Xiaoyuan's leather shoes tapped and squeaked on the cement floor, then she stood up.

"I'm not going to write a self-criticism," she said, "but I will tell you now that Zhuzhu's mother was a prostitute and her father was a bandit. I've seen her meeting up with loads of boys by the wharf, and it's me you want to write a self-criticism? Why aren't you getting her to write one?"

She finished what she had wanted to say in one breath and then she fled the office without permission, the angry calls of the headmaster and her teacher following behind her back. She knew she was already in trouble, but she could not contain this burning desire to get back at them. All the time she ran she heard her heart leaping, something sticking in her throat, suffocating her. She stood on the playground retching onto the lawn, yet nothing came out of her mouth but spittle.

Xiaoyuan's misfortune came about in this way.

A disciplinary action notice was pasted on the wall of Red Flag Middle School, and the one to be punished was none other than the famous Toon Street beauty He Xiaoyuan. On the second day after the notice was posted, the headmaster made a call to the Paean Photo Studio to demand that the photo of Xiaoyuan be removed from their window; he informed the photographer that this photograph had disturbed the school's order, and that it had caused the board considerable trouble. He demanded, from this moment forth, that the other party not carelessly display pictures of his students. The photographer didn't know how to feel about all this, but he cooperated with the headmaster's desires. The photograph of Xiaoyuan was quickly removed.

After that, Xiaoyuan became uncommunicative. She didn't try to ingratiate herself with a new group of friends, nor did she return to the clique led by Miao Qing. They were already close to graduation by that time, girls and boys alike, and Xiaoyuan conducted the remaining days of her education alone. According to policy, half of them would be sent to the countryside or to farms, and half of them would remain in the city. From the moment of that decision onward, every little group was disintegrated and replaced with two factions as different as the waters of the Jing and Wei rivers. Those who were going to the country squeezed together in the corridors every day, speaking of a future life which was so strange and distant from their own. Those who would remain in the city carried on playing dominoes, Zhuzhu in their centre, revelling in each other's happiness. Xiaoyuan stayed in a lonely corner, eating sunflower seeds or deep in thought. Xiaoyuan didn't want to talk with any of the other girls, and none of the other girls wanted to talk with her.

It was an early September morning when the trucks in red and green arrived on Toon Street to take them away. All the girls who were going to the countryside were gathered there, the beauty who lived beside the chemical factory among them. I saw her standing on the back of one of the trucks, a red flower on her chest, a striking contrast beside her pale melancholy. She did not cry like the other girls, but she didn't shout bold political slogans either. Xiaoyuan just leant on the side of the truck, quietly sweeping her eyes over the crowd of people that had come to see them off on their

journey. She saw Zhuzhu. The other girl was running after
the truck, waving a handkerchief in her hand. She knew,
really, that Zhuzhu had come to say goodbye to Li Qian but
that handkerchief had been Xiaoyuan's gift to her. Now,
Xiaoyuan wanted to ask for it back, as if Zhuzhu could hear
her amidst the sound of drums and cheering, as if Zhuzhu
would acknowledge the request even if she did. Xiaoyuan
was a sixteen-year-old girl, and so she understood sixteen-
year-old girls best of all.

The truck drove slowly, on past the entrance of the
herbal medicine shop where Xiaoyuan discovered that Crazy
Lu wasn't there. Odd, she thought, that he would not be
there on such a lively day. She was puzzled, and then she
turned to the boy next to her.

"Where is Crazy Lu these days? Do you know where
he's gone?"

The boy strained to hear her question, then used his
hand to amplify his reply, conveying the astonishing news
through the din of the crowd:

"Crazy Lu is dead. He ate so much medicine every day
that it killed him."

Xiaoyuan was sent to work on a farm in the remote
north. After five years she returned to Toon Street, and after
five years her snow-white face had become swarthy and
coarse. When she walked now, she swayed her shoulders like
a man, carrying her luggage down a Toon Street on which
none could recognise her as the beauty who lived beside the
chemical factory.

Only Zhuzhu recognised her immediately. It was a
chance encounter on the stone bridge, one that made them
both feel very awkward. Zhuzhu came down, Xiaoyuan

climbed up. They said nothing, and then after walking a few steps Zhuzhu turned her head only to discover that Xiaoyuan, too, had stopped at the other end. The two women gazed at each other in this way, separated by half the span of the stone bridge. It was Zhuzhu who broke the unbearable silence:

"I work at the Paean Photo Studio, come and get your picture taken sometime."

"I don't like having my photo taken, you'd better take a few more yourself." Xiaoyuan smiled wryly, touched her armpit and said: "I have body odour, and you're as pretty as an angel. Do you know it? You're still fair and all grown-up, you're as pretty as an angel."

V

Porcelain Factory
Shuttle Bus

开往瓷厂的班车

AT AROUND SEVEN IN THE MORNING, all of the porcelain factory workers from the northern part of the city would already be waiting at Huazhuang for their shuttle bus to arrive. There were seven or eight in total, all of them middle aged and wearing the blue overalls which were that factory's uniform, their lunchboxes and enamel teacups carried in nylon mesh bags. Seven or eight people hurrying one after the other to the station from the north, the south and the paddy fields. Usually speaking, once everybody had arrived the bus would arrive too; an old sky-blue thing coming down the road, swaying as it went with something always banging around inside. The heads of those seven or eight people twisted to the right in unison and one of them put her hands over her ears. The reason why quickly became apparent, the bus had difficulty stopping. When the driver applied the brakes the noise was as harsh as an ornithological scream.

The driver, the first to spot the two young strangers, removed his gloves to wipe water from the windshield. They had suddenly come running up from behind, waving their hands as they did, shouting: "Wait, wait for us!"

The driver turned his head to address the factory workers behind him. "Who are they? Does anybody know them?" The factory workers all stood up and looked at those two people.

"They aren't from our factory," they said. "They're probably Huazhuang people wanting a ride to the hospital."

"They're not Huazhuang people," the driver said. "Just look at their clothes, do they look like farmers? They're probably hitchhikers, don't let them on!"

But the strangers were running so fast that the tallest had already squeezed his body onto the bus by the time the driver could close the door. He stood there in the doorway and sighed with relief before shouting to the shorter one behind:

"Hurry up, you run like a hen!"

When the short one had also caught up, the two of them stood in the doorway together and offered a courteous wave to the other people on the bus. For their part, the porcelain factory workers surveyed the newcomers with curious or hateful glances; it was obvious that they were strangers. Their jean jackets were hanging around their waists, their high-topped sneakers were white, and fashionable silk scarves had been tied around their necks.

"What are you doing?" the driver asked, continuing to drive the bus forward as he spoke. "This is the factory shuttle, not a normal passenger bus."

"I know it's a factory shuttle," said the taller stranger as he selected a window seat. "It's the porcelain factory shuttle, right?" He looked at the driver with a relaxed smile in the corners of his mouth. "If it's the porcelain factory shuttle then we're on the right one," he said, shifting a little in his seat. Then he added: "We're going to start work there."

"You don't believe us?" asked the short one, sitting beside the taller one with an arrogant expression on his face. "We're new hires. If you don't believe us, you can go and ask the payroll department."

With a glance at the factory workers behind him which seemed to ask them to deal with it themselves, the driver said no more. It was then that Old Xu from the supply department remembered something.

"This year," he said, "the factory is hiring some new people, the kiln department needs new people."

It was obvious that Old Xu's words carried authority on

the bus. Everybody, including the driver, wore an expression of relief until they saw the shorter stranger flash a thumbs up to Old Xu, the gesture inspiring universal aversion. But nobody quarrelled over it.

"In that case," they said to the driver, "drive on."

And so, the porcelain factory shuttle went on its way. Its route had not changed for many years; from Huazhuang it would go through farmland then past the execution ground, on past the brick and tile factory and then a state-run forestry, more farmland, then a duck farm, farmland, a special petroleum plant, then farmland again. They would arrive at the porcelain factory about half an hour after they had embarked.

In the midst of the fine rain, the factory shuttle bus came hurtling over the bridge towards Huazhuang. Today those waiting for it noticed that it was accompanied not just by its customary din, but by those two young men. The tall one ran like he was trying to compete with the car and the short one, with great effort, ran after him while wrestling to open an umbrella. When the people at the station realised that the short one was trying to shield the tall one with his umbrella, they laughed at his excessive courtesy.

As the crowd moved in a damp huddle onto their bus, they saw the short one take the lead, occupying the seat next to the door. Here, he said to the tall one while packing up his umbrella:

"If we sit here, we'll be able to see the most clearly!"

What it was that the short one wanted to see the most clearly the factory workers did not know, what they did know was that every one of them hated the short one. Old Xu said:

"You, what's your surname? I reckon you don't even have your own, you just take his like a faithful dog." The short man took offence at Old Xu's hostility and said:

"Watch your fucking bullshit." After cursing so gratuitously, he turned back to talk to the tall one, who smiled proudly and said:

"Didn't you hear? Everyone says that you've got my last name, everyone says that you're my loyal dog!" The short one used the umbrella to jab the tall one in the leg and said:

"Watch your fucking bullshit. I'm serious, three people are going to be shot to death at the execution ground today. Seven o'clock, just wait a minute and I'll show you!"

As everyone listened to him speak, they became firmly convinced that everything that came out of the short boy's mouth was absolute nonsense. Their factory shuttle passed by the execution ground every day, yet never had they seen anybody facing the firing squad. They all knew that the place used to be an execution ground, but not any more. Since ancient times, these kinds of places have been avoided yet nowadays the execution ground grew closer and closer to Huazhuang, it's inappropriate.

"Seven o'clock. Three people shot to death." The short one's unbelievable news made everyone quite restless. At five minutes past seven, the porcelain factory shuttle bus passed the execution ground with every face within it peering out of its windows. Through the glass, they could make out a few trees and plants growing in the ground's rocky hollow, a fine drizzling rain falling among them. They saw a few birds fly into the air. Other than this there was nothing to see at all. It was just as they had expected; there were neither tethered prisoners on death row nor people waiting to pull the trigger. The execution ground would not live up to its name.

Letting out a snort from his nose as he spoke, Old Xu declared that this place had not been an execution ground for a very long time. Old Xu had barely finished speaking these words when the other factory workers hurriedly got back to their seats, embarrassed that they had fallen for the idle nonsense of a young boy. They sat as if they had never stood.

"In this weather, how could anybody be shot?" came a woman's voice. "The bullets would be damp."

The bus continued on its journey, tranquillity resuming over the vehicle until the factory workers suddenly heard the short one say:

"It was wrong, the time was wrong. It was seven o'clock that they had to shoot them, and they couldn't wait." The tall one pinched his nose tightly, releasing it and then grasping it tightly again before making a string of strange noises. Suddenly, he smiled darkly and said:

"I saw it, I saw it clearly. Three people tied up on their knees, then three bullets, and three people turned into three dead dogs!"

The short one turned his face to survey the other passengers from the corner of his eyes.

"They would have heard it," he said, "they would have heard the gunshot while they were waiting for the bus, but they weren't paying attention. Today three people were shot at seven o'clock, it was right there, three people were shot."

Old Xu gave the other passengers a wink which meant, are you all hearing the nonsense that comes out of this boy's mouth, lying even with all the facts in front of him! The passengers gave Old Xu a smile which meant, don't expose him yet, let's see how far he can get into the lie.

"A gun isn't that loud anyway," the short one said. "A machine gun's crack is just like frying beans, a little louder than frying beans, but executioners use automatic rifles. The sound of an automatic rifle is really clear, but if they had a muffler, the sound would be dull."

"You're fucking amazing," said the tall one. "So which guns were used? Missiles and rocket launchers too?"

"I'm not kidding you," the short one said. "Those three people are dead, it's just that this lot didn't hear it, their ears are no better than a deaf person's."

This was more than Old Xu could handle.

"Who are you calling deaf?" he said. "How could such a young man say these things? Show some respect!"

As they passed the duck farm the short one suddenly sprang out of his seat to the doors.

"Stop the bus," he said to the driver. "Stop the bus, stop now, I'm taking him to the execution ground, we'll see whether or not there's a bloodstain, and then we'll really know whether or not people were killed!"

"I'm not stopping this bus for you," the driver said. "What are the two of you up to, what workshop do you belong to?"

The tall one stayed in his seat, looking at his companion, clearly impressed.

"What workshop are you from? Oh?" he said. "Jump from the window, if you jump I'll jump too, if I don't jump I'm a dog. If I don't jump, you can ride on me while I crawl all over the road."

The passengers all looked at the short one, who grumbled a little but returned to his seat. As before, the two youths sat squeezed next to each other. Suddenly, the short one leaned forward and faced the window to cry out:

"Fuck, look at all these ducks!"

These two new factory workers were very strange. Once, Old Xu saw the two of them sitting smoking out on a pile of waste in front of the warehouse, but by the time he had passed the two men had already gone, the only evidence of them having been there at all was the cigarette butts on the ground. They have been here for ages, Old Xu thought to himself, puzzled. How can the kiln have hired two such young people to join the factory? Why is nobody minding them?

Old Xu thought that the two of them were very strange. On the fifth day of their appearance at Huazhuang station, Old Xu wanted to raise a lot of questions, but what disappointed him was that they didn't want to answer. They didn't respect him at all.

"What do you two do after work? How come I don't see you on the bus back?"

"We run home," the tall one said. "We have a competition, by the time I'm back at Huazhuang he still isn't even at the fertilizer plant. He runs like an old hen."

"What do you do at the kiln?" enquired Old Xu, his voice taking on the airs of a cross examination, who is the manager of the kiln?"

"And who are you?" said the short one, looking at Old Xu as he spoke. "You're Lu Guisheng aren't you? Meddling in everything as if your jurisdiction spreads wider than the Yangtze River.

At the mention of the name Lu Guisheng, which belonged to the factory director, Old Xu asked no more but only thought to himself, could they really be connected with Lu Guisheng? If so, I really have been meddling too much. Old Xu watched their backs, one tall, one short, and finally could not help himself but tap the shorter one on the shoulder.

"Hey, lad, he said. "What's your name?"

The short one moved his shoulder out of the way, avoiding Old Xu's hand.

"Hey, hey," he said. "Don't get fresh with me now, OK?"

Old Xu withdrew his hand and awkwardly turned to his colleagues.

"He says I'm getting fresh with him! I ask his name and he says I'm getting fresh!"

The short one still did not turn to look at Old Xu.

"What's with all these questions?" he asked. "Are you the census taker? Any name you can think of isn't mine, I don't have a name."

Old Xu wore an embarrassed smile and said:

"You don't have a name. Do you all hear that? He says he has no name."

The tall one turned this time to give Old Xu a wry look.

"He's just kidding you," he said. "He has a name. He's called Whole Is Red, just like the slogan from that stamp, *The Whole Country is Red*. His surname is Whole, his first name is Is Red."

After he had finished speaking the tall one hit the short one with his fist and laughed. The short one fought back with both fists before finally pointing at the tall one and saying to Old Xu:

"His surname is Rotten and his first name is Yellow Fish. Rotten Yellow Fish. Can you remember that?"

All the passengers started to laugh, but not Old Xu.

"This isn't a name," he said. "Are they your nicknames?"

The tall one turned his head and fixed Old Xu with a smirk.

"A name is a nickname," he said. "A nickname is a name."

They don't remember on which day this happened, just that it was the same day that the porcelain factory shuttle bus broke down next to the duck farm. The vehicle stopped by the side of the road while the driver looked to see how to fix it.

"It'll be fixed in a while," he said. The factory people were used to this kind of thing. Two women took knitting yarn out of their bags and Old Xu used the opportunity to urinate by the side of the road. He saw the two youngsters follow him as he jumped down from the bus.

The passengers all remember that they saw the two youths standing by the side of the road, the tall one twisting his waist and the short one moving his head about with his hands in a funny way. The workers watched the boys, the boys watched the duck pond.

Early autumn sunlight shone onto the surface of the pond. There were thatched houses, many ducks, and the keepers themselves were there far away, holding their duck whistles and looking at the road. The workers were used to the scene, they just sat quietly on the bus waiting for it to start moving again. After about ten minutes had passed, the driver emerged onto the bus with his face covered in grease.

Somebody asked: "Was it the spray nozzle?"

"It was the spray nozzle," replied the driver. "That old problem."

When the bus had gone on a little while, Old Xu let out a sudden exclamation – we've left them behind! The passengers quickly realised that they had indeed left behind the two young men. The driver stopped the bus.

"Eight people," he said. "I'm used to only counting eight people and I've gone and forgotten them. The passengers stood to look across the forest, farmland and pond which lay between them and the duck farm. They could make out the distant silhouettes of the two youths, one tall and one short, moving towards the duck keepers in the morning sunlight. Puzzled, the driver asked what they were playing at?

The passengers replied, "Who knows? Those two lads!" The driver wanted everybody's opinion:

"Shall I turn round and get them?" After a moment's hesitation the passengers responded in unison:

"Don't bother about them, let them go where they want!"

And so, the porcelain factory shuttle bus carried those same eight people as before as it went shaking towards the factory. What nobody expected was that the next day the two youths would not come to board the bus. It waited for them for three to five minutes at Huazhuang, but the two boys just didn't come. Everybody was full of uncertainty; their quiet and hardworking journey to and from the factory had never been disturbed like this before.

It was Old Xu who first began to investigate the two

youngsters' identities. The world fears earnestness, and the shifty fear the conscientious.

"You won't believe me when I tell you," said Old Xu, who had been rushing about the administrative offices and workshops, "that the short and tall lads weren't really porcelain factory workers at all! The payroll office doesn't know who they are!"

They could not believe him when he told them.

"Old Xu," they asked, "then what were they doing getting on the shuttle bus that early every day? What were they up to?"

Old Xu couldn't say why and so he said:

"Who knows? You'd have to ask them that yourselves."

The porcelain factory shuttle bus still takes the same old route as before, the same journey, but the names of the places through which it passes and even the scenery itself have shifted around its path. The bus has changed, too. You can see that the factory's profits have grown by looking at the brand-new Toyota shuttle. You can see that the factory workers' wages have grown from the increase in the number of people riding in it. Huazhuang has changed, it has innumerable tall buildings and a new overpass with cars flying over; it's flourishing. Even its name on the bus stop has been changed to *Huazhuang New Residences*. The porcelain factory shuttle bus goes from Huazhuang New Residences and passes the New World Playground, the Luyuan Park, the Jinfan Rihua Group, the Jinfan New Residential Area, an aquaculture plant, and then the Meihua Grand Hotel before arriving at the porcelain factory where you learn that it was renamed Gleaming Porcelain, Inc two years ago. The porcelain factory has about forty workers, thirty of which take the bus every day. Other than Old Xu, who sometimes mentions the execution ground, the farmland, the duck farm, nobody is interested in that kind of memory.

This story is really about something that happened on the day of Old Xu's retirement. It was a sunny autumn day again, and Old Xu emerged from the porcelain factory with the knowledge that, as today was a special day, he couldn't wait for the afternoon shuttle home. He crossed the road to wait at the ordinary bus stop where he could take a public bus home. But despite the heavy traffic of buses on the road, not one of them was destined for Huazhuang. After waiting impatiently for some time, Old Xu decided that since today was a special day, he would get a cab home. How much could a cab be? He stuck out his hand and within moments a red Xiali car had stopped in front of him.

It will be no surprise to anybody what happened next. Old Xu had bumped into somebody, one of those young men from all those years ago, the taller one, the one who had been called Rotten Yellow Fish. Old Xu was quite old, but his eyes were still sharp enough to recognise Rotten Yellow Fish the moment he saw him. He recognised Rotten Yellow Fish at a glance but, as we know, important people have short memories, and his face was blank. Old Xu patiently prompted his memory, and when Rotten Yellow Fish finally recalled, the memory seemed to make him uncomfortable. He waved his hands in front of him and said:

"Oh, I was just mucking about in those days, just muddling along."

Unsatisfied with this answer, Old Xu said:

"Why did you take our factory shuttle bus every day? It was such a long way, and I know you did nothing at all at the factory."

Rotten Yellow Fish thought for a moment and said: "I don't know why we went to the porcelain factory, just because we had nothing to do."

Old Xu's face was still full of doubt, so Rotten Yellow Fish tittered:

"You don't believe me? There's nothing I can do about that, we were just messing about, we didn't have a goal."

Old Xu shook his head and said:

"That can't be right, you weren't children. How can you have just been playing?"

Rotten Yellow Fish looked like he was getting impatient himself as he replied:

"If you don't believe it, that's up to you." A hint of anger tinged his voice.

"We didn't rob you or steal from you, did we? What harm did we do, riding on that bus?"

The taxi was faster than the shuttle, and so Huazhuang's tall new buildings were already rising unsympathetically on the other side of the window but Old Xu still had something he had to ask Rotten Yellow Fish. Old Xu took the opportunity to ask his most pressing question.

"Your friend, the short one? What's he doing now?" Old Xu watched as a strange smile developed on the other man's face and he said: "Why are you smiling?" What's he up to now? Is he a cab driver too?"

Rotten Yellow Fish's eyes focused on the road ahead, he heaved a breath and drew back his lips to smile, saying:

"He was killed. Whole Is Red was killed."

Old Xu let out a sound of wonder. Then, his body leapt indescribably from his seat like a bullet as he said:

"We're here, stop the car!" The passenger twisted himself out of the red Xiali, he had no idea why he was so agitated. Rotten Yellow Fish wound down his window with one hand and watched Old Xu. Realising that he had not yet paid, Old Xu regained his composure and hurried to scoop his cash out of his pocket. He faced the window and asked:

"What did he do? What did he do to get killed?"

Rotten Yellow fish sorted the money, placed some chewing gum into his mouth, and asked Old Xu straight back:

"You tell me! You tell me what he did!"

Old Xu, dumbfounded, unconsciously grabbed out for the mirror as he saw Rotten Yellow Fish hit the gas pedal, but the red Xiali had gone, and Old Xu was left empty-handed. Old Xu had no time to say anything, but he yelled after the car:

"That Whole Is Red, he was good to you!"

VI

Yingtao

樱桃扑

ACCORDING TO THE MAILMAN Yin Shu, Fenglin Road is an unusual place to make the rounds. The street is formed by a long, steep slope with trees shading it all the way. It can be traversed from the clock tower at its apex all the way to its nadir within two minutes if you keep your foot off the brakes of your bicycle, but the mailman can usually turn back the way he has come before then. Beyond Fenglin Hospital there are only the very few windows and high walls of the hospital and medical college. The letters or newspapers in his delivery bag are almost always bound for the hospital itself.

The previous mailman had been young and short-tempered, and once as he came plummeting down Fenglin Road like a comet, he had knocked down an old man walking along with his cane. The post office naturally decided to replace him after that. This was how the slim, slow and deliberate figure of Yin Shu first appeared on Fenglin Road.

Yin Shu's body is in harmony with his personality, so deliberate in fact that there seems nothing to spare on his slender frame at all. Those who worked at the post office regarded Yin Shu as a freak. He never spoke to any of them, his cold and indifferent gaze was enough to reject any conversation that they might attempt, so they called him a freak behind his back, a freak with eccentric habits such as using a great deal of rubber bands as he sorted letters not by address or name, but by the colour and shape of the envelope, a hassle-inviting practice which caused a lot of underhand laughter from his spectators. There was also the fact that just before he set off on his rounds, and despite the fact that his green trousers were already the smallest size and so could not possibly need it, he used two wooden clips to alter their cuffs. But after all, Yin Shu is Yin Shu, and nobody meddled with his eccentricities, he had his way of going about his work, and that was of no concern to anybody else, just like the bar of yellow soap that he kept under lock and key in his drawer; he bought it with his own money, therefore it was for his own use.

Yin Shu has never cared about anybody else's opinion of him. Only he knows that his own eccentricity is nothing more than the type of isolation or solitude which people often write about in the papers. Yin Shu rode his bicycle past that ancient clock tower at a quarter to nine every morning, he saw the colourful sunlight glorious around the tower, noted how the clock hands were always stuck at ten minutes past seven, leaning forwards as he reached the top of the street, and after that he would stop to look back at steep Fenglin Road, full of parasol trees, red maple and cedar, peaceful and clean, with only the faint smell of medicine wafting in the air, a smell which filled Yin Shu with a sensation of peace and cleanliness. He enjoyed that peculiar delivery route, and only he knew it.

It was raining that morning and Fenglin Road's concrete surface looked slippery with water and fallen leaves, so Yin Shu dismounted to push his bicycle down the hill. He approached a door in the side of the hospital building, one that always remained closed, and noticed that it had begun to rot, there was already moss growing in the cracks in the wood, then it suddenly and slowly began to open.

A girl in a white nightgown emerged from within, approaching Yin Shu and his mail cart. He subconsciously twisted the bicycle's handlebars away from her, but the girl's graceful steps came to block his way once more. She was young and pale, with a melancholic expression which caused a thumping in his heart – he saw her withdraw her right hand from the wide sleeve of her white nightgown, her skin sparkling like jade, full with some kind of hope just like the look in her black, limpid eyes.

"What do you want?"

"A letter. Do you have a letter for me?"

"What's your name?"

"Bai Yingtao."

"What?"

"Bai as in 'white' like 'white snow', Yingtao as in 'cherry' like 'cherry tree'. Maybe the letter just has 'Yingtao' written on it, that's me. I'm the only person called Yingtao."

He thought that her name was both strange and pretty, but he said nothing as he searched rapidly through the envelopes in his mailbag, finding that none of them were addressed to somebody called Bai Yingtao.

"There is no Bai Yingtao here," he said. "I don't have a letter for you."

"How could you not have it?" The girl slowly withdrew her hand, a shadow of gloom sweeping across her beautiful face.

"How could you not have my letter?" she said. "I've been waiting for so long."

She stood there blocking his way just as before, so he rung the little bell.

"Give way," he said. "Let me get past."

He discovered then that the sound of the bell startled the girl so much that she immediately dashed back to the wall.

Yin Shu pushed his bike forwards a few steps in a flurry,

then turned his head just in time to see that white-clothed figure disappear back into the side door, the vines at the top of the door's lintel rustling and swaying as it closed. Yin Shu supposed that he had encountered something rather strange, but after thinking about it for a while concluded that there was no wonder somebody in the hospital might want to sneak out to go for a walk, or even just to see the street scenery, it probably happens all the time. Yin Shu concluded that the girl in the white gown must have been an in-patient, but could not guess at what illness it was that troubled her.

The autumn wind cooled, and silence fell over the cicadas of Fenglin Road. The horn-like leaves of the Chinese gum tree had already turned red, and the parasols' had started to fall. The ground was covered with damp leaves, pulled whirling into the air by the wind or lying to slowly rot on the road's surface. If one could view a Fenglin Road autumn from above, one would find that it was thoroughly adorned with layer upon layer of warm red. It was easy for a passerby to forget the existence of the hospital by their side as they neared those high walls, and easy for them to forget that therein lay the kingdom of sickness and death.

Yin Shu the mailman likes autumns on Fenglin Road.

The sound of the rotten leaves being crushed under his bike reached Yin Shu's ears with a sound not unlike that of people whispering. He looked around, seeing the vast expanse of the cool October sky and the old trees with new leaves standing beneath its immensity. At such times, Yin Shu felt that his breathing coincided precisely with that of the world, a poetic feeling in his heart, nobody understood the particular happiness that Yin Shu experienced in autumn, just like nobody understood his loneliness in the remaining three seasons. His heart's eccentricity belonged to him alone, he never had the desire to open it to anybody else's touch. He sang a popular northeastern song as he went, but his husky and tender singing came to an abrupt halt.

He saw the girl in the white nightdress again, leaning against the door with a vine pulled down from the top of the wall in her hands and with the appearance of somebody waiting for someone, but who? From her eyes, he quickly realised that he was the one she was waiting for.

Bai Yingtao, the name leapt from the recesses of Yin Shu's memory. He subconsciously twisted the bundle of letters addressed to Fenglin Hospital, but he didn't need to check, he remembered clearly that there were no letters addressed to Bai Yingtao, and there never had been any for her in his bag at all.

"Mailman, do you have a letter for me?"

"I don't," said Yin Shu, shaking his head. He wanted to avoid her, but her desolate and earnest expression prevented him from doing so. Yin Shu spread the envelopes out like a fan in front of him and said: "These are all the letters addressed to Fenglin Hospital, see for yourself, your name is Yingtao, but I don't have a letter for you."

"They all call me Yingtao."

The girl approached the letters and began to turn them over delicately with her slender, jade fingers. The same hope existed in the girl's voice as before, maybe they just wrote Yingtao on the front.

"There are none for Yingtao, you can see for yourself; there's no letter for Yingtao."

He heard the girl sigh with a deep bitterness, a sound which made him really look at her pretty face and crimson lips for the first time. Such a sound expressed the cruelty of years of frosts and gales, but this girl was both young and beautiful, her jet-black hair flowing about her with the glow of youth. Yin Shu watched her finger trace the wall, her eyes already full of sparkling tears. I don't have a letter for her, I never had a letter for her. He felt as if a gentle spring had melted the coldness in his heart, a boundless pity arose within him for this girl named Yingtao.

"You're always here waiting for the letter," said Yin Shu. "Can you tell me who it's from?"

"My mother, I've waited every day since last year, but she hasn't written."

Yin Shu was unclear about Yingtao's answer.

"You've been in the hospital for a long time," he said. "How could your mother not know? Has she not been to see you?"

"She's very far away, I know she misses me every day, and every day I miss her too, but why does she never write to me? I wait every day, why has she still not written to me?"

"Maybe she doesn't know your address, maybe her letters got lost on the way, these things happen all the time."

Yin Shu heard Yingtao's whimpering sobs grow gradually more distinct. The autumn sun, fragmented and sparkling above the shade of the wall's vines, fell onto the girl's face and white nightgown, her every movement tinged with a sadness which seemed deeper than the ocean.

"Be patient and wait a little longer," said Yin Shu. "Maybe your mother's letter is already on the way." He shuffled the envelopes about uneasily in his hand, not knowing how to comfort her. He coughed before asking: "Other than your mother, who else could send you a letter?

If you tell me, I can keep an eye out for it. Who else is there?"

"Dachun, Dachun should have sent me one long ago. He knows I'm here." The girl used her wide white sleeve to cover her face and the tears in her eyes seemed to change in meaning. "Dachun, he ought to write, I gave him everything and I've suffered so much for him. Others can forget me, but never him, but why has he still not written to me?"

"I don't know, perhaps his letter was lost in the mail, too."

As Yin Shu said this, he saw a white ambulance hurtling at great speed down the slope of Fenglin Road, turning into the large gate of the hospital, its arrival reminding him that he had to complete his morning deliveries.

"I need to deliver these letters," he said, looking toward the girl with the trace of an apology as he spoke. Her white nightgown floated around her in the breeze, but the wind had not carried away her tears. Yin Shu pushed his mail cart forwards a few steps before turning his head to say:

"It's cold out, you ought to wear something a little warmer."

The staff at the post office noticed subtle changes in Yin Shu after that, the most obvious being that every now and then a smile would appear on his lips, making them guess that he had found a woman. Every day, Yin Shu broke the pattern of his normal behaviour to help those who worked in the sorting room at their task. He was still unwilling to speak, but they quickly discovered that he had an ulterior motive; he was looking for a letter. One day somebody bluntly asked:

"Yin Shu, whose letter are you looking for?"

Yin Shu hesitated a while before saying:

"Has anybody seen a letter addressed to Bai Yingtao? It would be addressed to Fenglin Hospital." Somebody probed further, asking:

"Who is Bai Yingtao? Is she your girlfriend?"

As soon as he heard this vulgar question, Yin Shu lowered his head and said no more, and the smile on his lips appeared haughty and mysterious.

Yin Shu was still Yin Shu, and that chance autumn meeting was his alone to know about.

Autumn is the season of damp fallen leaves, where the nocturnal rains come to wash the darkened city, ridding the deciduous trees of their dead. Yin Shu remembered that the girl always appeared in the mornings after a rain, her white nightgown and her body leaning against the wall emitting the smell of rain and leaves, wet, cold and poetic.

The girl was waiting for him again, wearing that same white nightgown as always in the autumn chill, clean as fresh snow. Yin Shu walked towards the girl, his attitude towards this unusual engagement a mixture between hope and fear. There was no letter, there was still no letter for her. He was closer to her now, but was too sorry to look her in the eyes.

"I don't have a letter for you," said Yin Shu, his feet kicking lightly at the rotten leaves. "Don't worry," he said. "Just be patient and wait a little longer."

"No, I've already run out of patience."

The girl's voice seemed to have lost the grief of before, as she stood there between the door and the hanging vine, combing though her long hair with her fingers. Yin Shu felt her eyes on his face for a while. He lifted his head, her limpid eyes like autumn rain were deep and clear with a loving tenderness.

"I'm not waiting for a letter," she said. "I'm just waiting for you."

Yin Shu was unable to understand her meaning for a long time. He scratched his head.

"Why are you waiting for me? If you're not waiting for a letter, then what's the use in waiting for me?"

"I want to talk to you."

The girl pulled a vine from the wall, plucking at its slender leaves, every one of her tiny movements giving the impression of refined grace.

"I want to talk to you," the girl said. "Nobody will talk to me in the hospital, none of them like to speak. I get depressed so quickly, I'm mad with loneliness."

The girl's behaviour took Yin Shu by surprise, leaving him with a feeling that the affair had taken a sudden change.

"Talk? Just to talk?"

Yin Shu looked at the girl awkwardly, forcing a little laugh and said:

"As it happens, I don't like to talk, either."

"But every time I sneak out, I see you."

"You're a patient, you ought to speak with the doctors," said Yin Shu. "You need to speak with the doctors, why don't you go and speak with them?"

"They never listen to me, they don't want to listen to me. You're not the same as them. I think you're the only one I can talk to. You're the only good person in the whole world."

"Why do you say that? You don't really know me."

"No, I know you." The girl suddenly smiled and lowered her head to look at the white nightgown which clothed her.

"I wear it in all four seasons, the cold, the wind, the snow. I often feel cold, and not once has anybody told me that it's cold, that I ought to wear something warmer, only you."

Yin Shu's face felt indescribably hot.

"It really is cold," he stammered. "Why are you still wearing that gown?"

"Because it is all I have. I have nothing else. I have more sad things I want to tell you. Do you want to listen?"

"I want to listen, but I'm a mailman, I need to deliver mail."

Yin Shu noticed the girl's face once again show sorrowful resentment and disappointment, and her eyes flowed with glistening tears in an instant. Yin Shu wanted to stay, and he wanted to go. He thought for the right wording, and then finally said:

"Tell me your ward number! I'll visit you when I have a day off."

"Ward nine, bed number nine. Easy to remember," said the girl, turning her face to look at the high walls of the hospital, using a sort of melancholic sound as she repeated it:

"Ward nine, bed nine, you can't forget a promise, you will come and see me."

"I never forget a promise," said Yin Shu. "I will certainly be back to see you."

Yin Shu pedalled his cart a few metres before he felt a breeze, a string of steps behind him and the girl had over-taken him, obstructing his way as she gazed fixedly at him with a strange expression.

"What?" Yin Shu was forced to stop. "I'm not lying to you," he said. "I'll come to see you."

"I believe you." The girl's expression suddenly became bashful, she lowered her head to say: "Can you give me something? Anything at all, just as long as it's something you have on you right now."

"Anything at all?" he asked doubtfully. He first touched the mailman's cap on his head, then the key in his coat pocket, thinking that nothing was appropriate, then said regretfully: "I'm so sorry, but I'm wearing my work clothes right now, and I don't have anything else suitable on me.

"Anything at all. I don't want a present, I just want something that's yours."

The girl's voice seemed parched and sincere.

Finally, Yin Shu pulled a handkerchief out of his pocket of the type often used by men, grey and blue checkered.

"How about this handkerchief? It's a little dirty, but it's all I have."

Yin Shu remembers the look of happiness and satisfaction on the girl's face. She grabbed the handkerchief and fled back into the hospital's side door like a white deer, his last vision of her was of her waving that handkerchief all the way as she went, the handkerchief fluttering gracefully in the breeze as did her nightgown, all flowing together in the October breeze.

On the bright days to come, when Yin Shu came to deliver his letters to Fenglin Road he noticed that the door to the side of the hospital was shut tight, its rust and moss serving as testament to its abandonment.

The girl in the white nightgown did not sneak out again, a fact which Yin Shu thought was very strange. As he gazed at the door where he was used to seeing her, his heart became listless.

. . .

Yin Shu didn't forget his promise. Early one Sunday morning, he changed his green mailman's uniform for regular attire and entered Fenglin Hospital. The old person at the reception desk recognised Yin Shu and said:

"Have you come to visit a patient?"

Yin Shu nodded his head, but offered no explanation, he just wore that haughty and mysterious smile.

The hospital is very big, and so a man who almost always walks upon a lawn of fallen leaves found himself walking in circles along the winding corridors reeking of disinfectant. Yin Shu began to feel apprehensive. He was a mailman, so he was good at recognising addresses, how was it that he could not find Bai Yingtao? Where was ward nine? As two nurses rushed past him, he asked:

"Where is the ward nine?"

Their reply shocked him so much that he thought he was in a dream.

"We don't have a ward nine," said one of the nurses. "It was turned into a morgue long ago."

The other nurse pointed to the wood grove behind the hospital, saying:

"There's a building with a red tiled roof in there, that's the morgue."

Yin Shu does not remember how he made it to the building with the red tiled roof, nor does he remember where he got the nerve to do so. A hospital worker was repairing a stretcher at its door with a clanging noise.

"Is there a girl called Bai Yingtao here?" Yin Shu asked him.

"Yes," said the worker. "I think she's in number nine."

"Do you know when she died?" asked Yin Shu.

"In the summer," replied the worker. "She's been there ever since, nobody came to collect her, that girl never had any idea what was going on. Who are you to her?"

"I'm nothing to her," said Yin Shu, "I'm a mailman, I just want to see her."

The colour drained out of Yin Shu's face, his heart falling deeper into the pit of his stomach with each step towards number nine. He saw that girl in the white nightgown, her beauty as if she were alive, her lonely expression the same as before. Yin Shu saw the girl's pale jade hand, saw how tightly it grasped his handkerchief.

VII

Grey Woollen
Peaked Cap

灰呢绒鸭舌帽

THE PEAKED CAP on Old Ke's head was made of ash-grey wool, looking like an object with quite a history. In fact, the truth of its origin was simply that it was bought by its wearer's father, who had been an elegant dandy of a man in his youth with a particular penchant for collecting a variety of trendy hats. This one, in particular, had been casually purchased in an imported-goods store in old Shanghai. It was made of only the finest materials, especially the interior, which comprised soft foam and Scottish cotton, making it feel exceedingly snug on his shiny bald head.

While Old Ke's father was alive, he had loved to wear that grey peaked cap most of all. On his deathbed, he had given it to his only son. Old Ke remembers that his father had asked him to bend down to him, so he had bent down, then his father's ice-cold and trembling hand had sought the space on the top of his son's head. Stroking it, he said:

"You're beginning to lose your hair."

After that, Old Ke saw a gratified smile float across the old man's face as he lifted the ash-grey woollen cap from his pillow. With great difficulty but great resolution, the old man placed it onto Old Ke's head.

"This is a good cap, you wear it now."

These were the last words Old Ke's father whispered into his ear.

Old Ke remembers that his father got him to lean in close to his lips, pushing his right ear against the man's withered and blood-drained lips, and the result was that he heard that sentence: "This is a good cap, you wear it now." Old Ke, thinking that perhaps his father had hidden something in the lining, waited until he had ended his period of vigilance over his father's coffin to secretly prise apart the cap's interior.

Contrary to all expectations, he found nothing, nothing at all lay waiting within the cotton. Old Ke had no idea why his father would only give him a cap, so he treated this throwaway object with disdain. Old Ke thought even one pair of socks would be preferable to ten hats.

The hat was put into a chest. One autumn morning two years later, Old Ke woke up early to prepare breakfast for his wife and son when he gradually became aware of his wife watching him from behind. She was combing out her own beautiful long hair in front of the mirror but all the while staring at the back of his head with a strange and mysterious expression.

What are you looking at? Old Ke asked.

"I'm looking at your hair."

A warm smile suddenly appeared on her face. She used the wooden comb to point at him as she said:

"Your hair is getting thinner and thinner, it looks as if every day some of it is falling out. It's funny, it looks like..."

"Looks like what?"

"It looks like the sun in our son's drawings, rays of light coming out on all sides but in the middle totally empty, gleaming bald."

His wife puffed out a laugh. As she observed her husband's reaction, she discovered that his blank expression was becoming one of fury.

"Come here, I'll show you in the little mirror, have a look at your hair."

Old Ke stood between the two mirrors. In this way, he saw the back of his head for the first time. It was an exaggeration to say that it looked like the sun and the rays of light in one of their child's drawings but it was the exact image of his late father. And so, on this breezy morning Old Ke miserably came face to face with the destiny which mankind bequeaths to itself. In so few years, his head of lustrous black hair had disappeared like so many straws of hay in the wind; a cruel blow for even the least vain of men.

"I have a hat," he said solemnly to his wife. "I'll wear the hat to work." The hat to which he referred was that grey peaked cap.

That was how the hat found its way out of the chest's confines where it had been for two years. Old Ke's wife hung the hat outside the window so that the sunlight might dispel the musty smell that had seeped into it. As the sun dipped behind the mountains and the smell was all but gone, she took a needle and thread to repair the hole that had appeared in its lining.

On Toon Street, the men are simple and unadorned dressers, very few of them wear hats, no matter what the season. It was for this reason that Old Ke's appearance seemed quite unusual, and the hat became a symbol of his. Everybody noticed it from afar, often calling him from a distance with the cry:

"Old Ke, have you shaved your head?"

Certainly, this is a commonly shared joke between men, and Old Ke didn't make a fuss over their jeering remarks. You're not proud of your thick hair, he thought to himself, and neither is it a shameful thing to be bald, it's nothing more than a matter of individual physiology. However, in Old Ke's heart he knew that he really did have a problem with it. Every time he passed the barber's shop, he would turn his face away. Why do I turn my face away? Am I self-conscious, am I shy? His introspections discovered a certain type of loneliness that was difficult to put into words, a loneliness tainted by an unquenchable grudge; Old Ke discovered that he resented his father. If it were not for his father's genes, he too would be paying frequent visits to that barber's shop like every other man on Toon Street.

Autumn turned to winter, and in winter's freezing streets Old Ke began to see other men sporting hats as they went about their days. He noticed though that as their hair stuck out from under these hats in dense locks, they wore them simply to keep out the cold. So, despite the change, he felt just as solitary as before. In fact, the only thing he had to console himself was the quality of his own inherited cap; it stuck out as an icon of individuality and taste among all those crude work caps, military caps and old-style felt caps worn by other men.

I don't know exactly when it started, but one day Old Ke began to appreciate the cap that his father had left him. Indeed, it got to the point where he discovered that he could not do without it, even wearing it around the house in his own home. He would hang it on the side of the bed just before going to sleep and the first thing he did when he woke up was to pick it back up. This eccentricity of his began to annoy his wife and so, on one occasion, as he was reaching out for it, she pulled back his arm.

"I'm so tired of that hat", she said, unable to conceal her irritation as she spoke. "From morning 'til night you're always wearing it. I have never said I dislike you being bald, why is it that the first thing you do when you open your eyes is to grab that damned hat?"

"No," he said, "it's not like that. You don't understand, I've just got used to it. When I don't wear it now, I feel like I'm missing something."

"And what," his wife interrogated him, "are you going to do in the summer? You're still going to wear it in the hottest months?"

"I don't know, ask me when summer comes."

But Old Ke's wife would not accept this vague attempt at dismissing her enquiries. She asked him again, what are you going to do in summer? Old Ke really couldn't predict what he would do. He considered matters that arose later should be considered later. After autumn comes winter, whether or not I wear the hat in summer will be decided in summer.

Days passed one after the other, and beyond Old Ke's window Toon Street flowed past one drop of time after the next. That year, Old Ke was thirty-five. At thirty-five years old he had hardly any hair left at all. He vaguely remembered his father once making a prediction when he was alive that Ke men can't get past their thirty-fifth year without becoming bald; when you reach thirty-five, it'll happen to you, too. Sometimes, Old Ke would stand in front of the mirror and remove his cap, running his hands over his head to examine whatever strands remained from every angle. He discovered that in the past six months his hair loss had become all the more serious. He didn't know whether this was to be blamed on that grey cap itself, or whether it was simply his destiny to go on continuously losing hair? Old Ke lowered his head to gaze at the hat his father had left him. Suddenly, he felt that his hair and even his whole life was entirely under the control of his father and this hat he had inherited. Thinking it over, it was as if it was ordained by heaven.

Old Ke moved the cap around in his hands with a gentle and expert motion of his fingers. Sometimes it worried him but deep down he knew that he treasured it. No matter what, Old Ke would not be separated from his hat.

It happened on the eve of Grave Sweeping Day. The whole Ke family had piled into a truck filled mostly with people from Toon Street on their way to visit the public cemetery where they would sweep their family graves and offer their spirits incense, among them the happy racket of the children. Old Ke and his family were completely inconspicuous. It was as the truck pulled up before the empty space in front of the chemical plant that everybody heard his wife say: "Are you going to wear that hat to sweep your family's graves?" Old Ke rebuked her in front of everybody, impatiently avoiding her eyes as if furious, he said:

"You meddle in everything, if I take it off when we get there will that be the end of it?"

The route to the public cemetery took the truck along a long rural highway, paved haphazardly with stone in such a way that the truck frequently bounced over it. The children were all held in their mother's arms, sitting on the floor of the flatbed while the men stood, some of them enjoying the spring scenery and some chatting idly to each other. The wind was high that day and the men narrowed their eyes against the gale. Their hair and collars fluttered about them all as they stood. It was probably because of the wind. Everybody saw Old Ke's hat as it was blown so suddenly into the air it was as if an invisible hand had plucked it from his head. He cried out, subconsciously lifting his hand to grab at the hat but he only grazed its brim. Everybody on the truck raised their heads to look at the hat, watching as it began to glide towards the ground after a short instant in the air. What shocked them was Old Ke's reaction. They all saw him leap over the truck's fender, snatching at the hat. It was with this strange posture that Old Ke fell to the highway.

It had all happened in an instant. Old Ke's wife had fainted from shock and the truck had turned back towards the city, the men not too shocked to act promptly by taking the injured man to hospital. By that time, Old Ke was already too weak to talk; he could only weakly lift his hand to the people at his sides, asking for something. The hat, somebody said, he wants the hat. It was in this way that the grey wool hunting cap finally made its way back into Old Ke's grasp.

He struggled in that hospital ward for a full day but the hue of death which had climbed into his face remained. His wife brought his son to his bedside and when she saw that hat still grasped firmly in his hand she suddenly blamed everything on the object. She tried to pull it away from him but his fist was too tightly clasped around it.

"This damned hat, it's all the hat's fault." The woman sobbed. At that, she saw an inexplicable smile move into her husband's face; he shook his head and finally let go of the cap. Old Ke turned his eyes to gaze at his child with a look full of tenderness, opening his mouth wide as if to speak but the words would not come. So his wife could only seek else-where for meaning.

"You want to give him the hat?"

Old Ke nodded his head, still opening his mouth as if to speak.

"You want to give it to him now? It's too big for him now. It won't fit now, don't you think?"

Old Ke shook his head. He raised his hand, looking like he wanted to touch his child's head but wasn't able to. Not because he was too weak to lift his own arm but because the child was too young to understand. With a shrill scream, he hid behind his mother in fear of the dirt and blood on his father's body.

The grey peaked cap slid from the hospital bed to the cement floor without a sound. Old Ke's wife bent to pick it up, brushing the dust away from it as she did. "I know what you mean, if his hair is like yours one day you want him to wear the hat." Old Ke's wife sobbed as she spoke. "No matter whether this hat is lucky or not, I'll do as you say."

She believed that she had understood her husband's final request but when she looked at him she found that he was faintly shaking his head. He shook his head until at last his breathing suddenly stopped. Old Ke's wife still didn't quite understand the dead man's wishes. This has been a pang in her heart throughout her life as a widow.

Many years have passed since Old Ke's death but it is still fresh in the memory of Toon Street's residents who have all been watching his son mature with great interest. That mischievous boy, pampered so much by his mother, has already grown big. Everybody calls him Young Ke.

Young Ke is often seen going to and fro on the street on his blue bike. His appearance, whether he resembles his father or his mother more, and particularly whether his hair resembles his father's or his mother's more, is a regular topic of conversation among the women who gather in front of the grocery store. This would appear to be a trifling matter but really it shows their neighbourly concern; they all remember the story of Old Ke's hair and Old Ke's hat and they all remember that it was a tragic and strange story.

The women outside the grocery store were unable to decide who the boy really resembled more so they decided that he looked like both of his parents which seemed like a logical conclusion. Young Ke was a handsome and fashionable boy and liked to tie a checkered scarf to his jacket but he never wore a hat. His style was certainly completely different to his father's, just as the era he lived in was like another world to the gloomy monotony of the sixties and seventies.

Young Ke's mother was a neurotic woman, so when he was asleep she often took the opportunity to secretly stroke his messy hair. This woke him up, so he had an aversion to the habit. Young Ke didn't know what was in his mother's heart. Young Ke's mother didn't know whether her son's hair would be like hers or his late father's, she didn't know whether, when the time came, he should inherit the Ke family's grey woollen peaked cap. Now, Young Ke is only twenty years old, who knows whether he will be bald like a monk at thirty-five? Even his own mother is unable to guess.

VIII

Cavalry

骑兵

My cousin is bow-legged. This means that regardless of what he does, his legs and knees just will not touch together. My uncle, Zuo Lisheng, blames this unfortunate condition on his son's childhood infatuation with a wooden rocking horse but I don't know whether there's any scientific basis to his theory. That rocking horse had been discarded by the district nursery back when my poor aunt, who was in good health at the time, was still working there. Knowing that it would be a relief for her husband, who was always being made to pretend to be a horse for the child's games, she used her position to be able to buy the enormous gift for five *mao* (50 *fen* or cents). I remember seeing it myself when I was small but I never got the chance to have a go. Zuo Lin would not let anybody else ride it. Its body was covered in shards of blue paint and the handles on both sides had already been gripped by so many children that they looked as greasy as the ears of a real-life horse. He would rock about on its back from dawn until dusk; he would eat on it, read his comics on it, sometimes when he was tired, he would even hold onto it as he slept. That is how selfish he was, he would rather hold onto the wooden horse in his sleep than let anybody else have a ride.

Zuo Lin was nine years old in the winter that my aunt got into a traffic accident at the nursery gates. She had been walking on the frozen street with two chamber pots full of children's urine when a truck crashed into her on its way to deliver coal to the nearby coal yard. It was like the tricks in the ghost stories which she would tell, where a demon could arise out of any object and, of course, would turn out to be skilled in the art of magic and deception. I do not know whether it was an evil trick of the chamber pot demon or the coal cinder demon that turned her into nothing. According to my parents' recollection, it was at my aunt's funeral that they all discovered that Zuo Lin's legs were abnormal; he couldn't kneel. When he knelt, each of his knees had a mind of their own. They would not close together at all but remained as far apart as if he were sitting cross-legged on the floor. Everybody was stuck between confusion and grief. There were some people who tried to straighten his legs a little but after being at it for a while they realised that it was useless and gave up, and who would dare discuss the shape of the child's legs on such an occasion. A long time passed before Zuo Lisheng took his son to see an orthopedic doctor. He pulled down his son's trousers and asked the doctor: "My son can't be bow-legged, can he?"

"Your son is bow-legged," said the doctor. Zuo Lisheng was anxious, waiting in the hospital for a specialist, but the doctor told him: "Your son's legs simply can't be straightened, and they don't need to be, either. The issue will not affect him beyond it looking unpleasant when he walks."

Zuo Lisheng trusted what the doctor said, but he was not going to blindly follow his advice. Convinced that the wooden horse had something to do with the curvature of his son's legs, he split it for firewood when he returned home. That day, Zuo Lin's screams drew half the street to their house. Faced with the destruction of that horse, the children's feelings were thrown into confusion. On one hand they thought it was a terrible pity but on the other they couldn't help but feel a little pleasure at someone else's misfortune. Meanwhile, the adults' efforts to soothe Zuo Lisheng just made him angrier.

"Horse riding, horse riding," said Zuo Lisheng, brandishing his firewood axe as he spoke, "horse riding causes bow-leggedness. I'm telling you, don't let your children ride horses, even wooden ones!"

Zuo Lin is bow-legged. We Toon Street children worshipped San Ba with the tiger tattoos on his arms, worshipped Ah Rong, who was missing his index finger, and even worshipped hare-lipped Fengshou the boxer; but nobody thought much of my cousin Zuo Lin. Everybody thought that whenever Zuo Lin walked, not only was it ugly but it was actually funny, and whenever he stood still it was like his legs were two pincers ready to clamp something between them. The thing was that if the shape really had come from riding a horse then we would have all revered him but Toon Street is not the prairies of Inner Mongolia. If you discounted a few cats and dogs, and Wang Deji who ignored the sanitation laws to raise his chickens, there was not so much as a little donkey to be found. In such a place, where even the local gangster San Ba had no horse to ride, what could Zuo Lin have ridden? The only thing Zuo Lin had to ride was an old bicycle that my aunt had left behind. He would take it out and ride it with the evening darkness as his shield but there was always somebody to start trouble with him anyway, reaching out to grab the bike.

"Get off, give me a go and you can chase me!" Some loved to make a fool of Zuo Lin. Others loved to watch Zuo Lin being made a fool of. They would make eyes at each other, the focus of their expression aimed at Zuo Lin's legs. As he stood in their field of vision, his two poor knees seemed like they were gasping for breath, gasping like desperate caged animals, and when he ran he would yell high, futile cries after the bicycle thief:

"Stop, stop the bike!"

His two knees also let out their own hoarse cries in succession until both sides of Toon Street rang with laughter in the twilight – you won't believe me when I tell you why everybody laughed when he ran but those knees really did have a voice of their own; they could shriek, they could even sob.

It would have been fine if Zuo Lin had been a tree, which never has any need to stand at attention and can grow just as crookedly as it pleases with nobody minding at all. But Zuo Lin is not a tree, he is a human being who can hear the order to stand at attention, an order which is no problem for the vast majority of people; everyone can stand at attention except my cousin Zuo Lin.

Zuo Lin didn't like attending gym class, nor aerobics, nor military training but in our school days your time was pretty much full of that sort of thing. To be fair, most of our teachers or group leaders handled Zuo Lin's particular situation with a particular response; when others stood to attention, he would stand at ease, and some would simply remove him from the otherwise orderly line. However, some people are just naturally distrustful, always nitpicking, and our school's gym teacher was one of them. He mistook Zuo Lin's kind of feigned, relaxed smile for mischievousness, suspecting that he was using his posture either to evade, vent or oppose something. He once dragged Zuo Lin to the lavatories, removing Zuo Lin's trousers to inspect his knees with his own hands when, in those quiet surroundings, he was stunned to hear the cry of the knees for himself. Squatting on the ground and using two fingers to tap at Zuo Lin's two legs, he stared as if in fear at Zuo Lin. "How can your knees make a sound?"

The corners of Zuo Lin's mouth betrayed a hint of self-satisfaction as the desire came over him to cross his legs, to stand in front of the gym teacher with his body twisted like a braid of fried dough. As Zuo Lin stood there saying nothing, his eyes clearly intent on flaunting something or other, the gym teacher heard the cry of the knees, a crackling, metallic shriek.

"How is that sound happening? Don't stand like that!" He was certainly frightened by Zuo Lin's knees and started to fix his posture in a flurry, saying: "Stop it, you're going to break your legs!"

Zuo Lin knew that no matter what, he could always rely on his knees to frighten a rude and presumptuous man, but his opportunities to do so were so rare that he felt an indescribable satisfaction whenever he did, feeling like some outside audience as he enjoyed the bountiful changes of expression on the other party's face, from shock to discomfort, from discomfort to pity and, all the while, he bit his fingers to hide his laughter. Afterwards the gym teacher sighed and said:

"You can't stand straight, I've mistreated you, but... but you'll never be a soldier with those legs." Zuo Lin pulled on his trousers indifferently and went to relieve himself where, facing the urinal, he said:

"Who wants to be a soldier!"

He turned his face to peep at the gym teacher who had been a soldier and whose military trousers radiated deep green light before Zuo Lin's eyes. The contours of a man's straight legs, the epitome of health, were faintly visible beneath them. It was in that instant that Zuo Lin's ears rang with other people's teasing: "Zuo Lin, you can be a cavalry soldier." All those different people imagined the same wonderful future for his legs, even the street thug San Ba would comfort him in that way – "Your legs are bent just like a cavalry soldier's, Zuo Lin, you're going to be in the cavalry!"

"I'm going to be in the cavalry." Zuo Lin stood in front of the urinal and, glancing from left to right, began to mutter to himself. Something had really got him thinking. The lavatory floor had been washed at midday and was half dry, half wet with autumn sunlight pouring in through the row of windows, creating a subliminal confusion between shadow and light, and water and urine, in which Zuo Lin suddenly saw the exact image of a galloping horse.

"I ride horses," he said. "I'm a cavalryman."

Zuo Lin stayed in the lavatory after the gym teacher had left, staring at the floor, watching as the galloping water stain began to dilate, undulate in the sunlight, began to rise further and further up. And then that magical thing happened, he heard the broken but aberrantly sweet sound of hoofbeats coming from the thicket outside so he raised his head to peer through the window and there he clearly saw it, the white, long-maned steed charging onto the playground from the depths of the shadows of the trees. And then there was a billboard in the way, and then when he emerged on the other side of the billboard, the white horse was nowhere to be seen, it had vanished more quickly than it had appeared, the sound of its final hoofbeat submerged beneath a wave of noise. Zuo

Lin saw the school's dirt playground unchanged, clouds of dust flying above it, arid September sunlight illuminating the lines of rehearsals for National Day, a woman's voice over a loudspeaker, repeating commands: "One, two, open – three, four, close." A wreath of people blossomed and unblossomed over the playground's surface according to the voice's commands. That white steed was gone. Restless, he concealed himself behind the billboard, doubting his own eyes, there could never have been a horse in the school. But Zuo Lin had not resigned himself to giving up on his miracle so he waited patiently, staring in the direction of every sound. However, the miracle did not appear again, and all he saw was the same school barracks, half peaceful, half raucous, the peaceful and the raucous in sharp confrontation. A golden dragonfly dashed against the glass of the billboard, a page of homework flew low in the air before tumbling into a flowerbed. That was not the miracle for which Zuo Lin was waiting. The white horse was nowhere to be seen. Utterly disappointed, Zuo Lin was unwilling to return to the playground but instead left the school as the rehearsal neared its end.

Usually, Zuo Lin would slink past the office window with his waist bent but today Zuo Lin needed to know for sure whether that white horse had been a miracle or a fantasy. He knocked on the glass to ask the old entrance guard:

"Did a white horse run into the school just now?"

"What white horse running into our school?" said the old man.

"A white horse," repeated Zuo Lin, "did you see a horse running into our school?"

The old man heard clearly that time and so, in a rage which Zuo Lin did not understand in the least and which was certainly caused by him believing that Zuo Lin was making fun of his eyesight, he grabbed a broom and thrust it out of the window.

"I don't see any white horse. I just see you, you black donkey!"

Many people harbour an intense hatred for Zuo Lin, who unconsciously opened the door and fled, remembering suddenly as he did so that the old man suffered from an eye disease. He would often have one wrapped in gauze and struggle to tell who was a teacher and who was a student. He still remembers that the old man chased him out of the office, swearing after him in a way that was at first indignant, then full of unexpected surprise as he said:

"Oh yeah, Zuo Lisheng's son! You want to make fun of me but I can see well enough to see you're a black donkey. Run away, run bow legs, how fucking fast you can go?"

It was not a rare thing for Zuo Lin to hear insults hurled in his direction so such insults rarely made Zuo Lin angry but they did make him very curious as to why people used all their wisdom and so much vocabulary to describe his gait. Some would say he walked like he was pissing, pissing while he walked, while others said that the blacksmith's big yellow dog could run straight through his crotch. Some were gentler and said he was like an Antarctic penguin. Then there were some Zuo Lin really resented, like Chungeng, who said he looked like a girl who'd just been raped by a Japanese devil! Zuo Lin ran down the twilit street, his knees emitting their usual voiceless shriek. Zuo Lin did not hear the sound of his own knees and was puzzled over why the old man would call him a black donkey. He had a faint recollection of seeing a war film in which a village woman had ridden a donkey into enemy territory. The donkey carried two bundles on its back, inside which were landmines. But that donkey's appearance was already blurred and what he saw as he ran was the same white horse as before, this time clearly conscious that it was a make-believe horse so it ran insanely fast while he watched himself astride it, hurtling past the narrow lines of people on Toon Street, everybody stopping to stare as his mouth let out the powerful rider's command: "*Ya, ya, ya.*" He made a whipping gesture toward the bike in front of him and sped away down the dusky street, like a horse, or like the cavalry.

In the autumn of that year, Zuo Lin lived his life on horseback according to his own cavalry fantasy. My mother once went to his house to take them some chicken soup and saw that he had heaped a pile of quilts onto three chairs, mounted the quilts and began to shrug his shoulders and move his legs. My mother said:

"Zuo Lin, what are you up to, you'll wear a hole in those quilts."

Zuo Lin has never been one for explaining his eccentricities to other people, he just sat on his ersatz horse eating his chicken soup.

"You're still kicking your legs about and getting soup everywhere, Zuo Lin," said my mother. "How come you're still playing little boys' games at this age?"

After my mother came home, she was in a sad state, worrying about how hard it would be for Zuo Lin to grow up without a mother, but what made her worry the most was how the boy would carry on as if there were nobody at all to see him, as if to suggest, I'm playing my little boys' games, and it's none of your business. Zuo Lin spent that autumn alone but for a burning and puzzling secret in his heart. Even I noticed his feverish obsession with cavalry; I once saw him riding on the school gate as if it was a horse, striking a majestic pose with his finger pointing up at the sky. His behaviour worried everyone, and they all called on Zuo Lisheng to pay attention to the child's developmental problem, but Zuo Lisheng would not listen, saying that only Zuo Lin's bones were askew, that his head was on straight, that he had a strange temperament, that people bully him and, anyway, so what if he wants to be a cavalry soldier? The blind become fortune tellers; the bow-legged become cavalry soldiers, that's their luck!

But Toon Street is in the south, and other than a few zoo zebras, animals that only eat and never run, you couldn't even find a halfway decent replacement among the cattle. You can well imagine the difficulty of achieving Zuo Lin's mounted dream. But Zuo Lin's mind was always on his horse. He was completely incapable of walking steadily down the street. As soon as he got to the road he would hear the *ta ta ta* sound of hooves, compelling him to trot at the gait of a soldier at the head of a military train, but he knew that the horse beneath him was not real. He removed the wooden handle from a sickle he had found at home and hung it from his waist as if it were a sabre, then in the same way as he found a substitute for the riding sabre, riding boots and riding whip; he found them all except for the most important riding thing, a miracle for which he waited all autumn, but the white horse never returned. Then early one morning, bright after the night's rain, Zuo Lin awoke to find his hungover father lying directly beneath him. In his dreams, he had climbed onto his father's back, leapt onto his father's back just like a cavalry-man. In that moment, Zuo Lin was confused and surprised, quivering gently behind his father. Zuo Lisheng had a soft but sturdy back, reminding his son of a strong horse. Zuo Lin was reluctant to leave, but he stood up to go to the bathroom when he heard his father begin to mumble in his sleep. In such a way, that wonderful sensation of riding ended and wouldn't come back. Zuo Lin knew full well that he wouldn't be able to jump onto his father's back again.

Everybody always says that art needs inspiration, and my cousin's inspiration came from that event. On that day, as the sunshine came to dispel the previous night's rain, he set about selecting a horse from the people.

Zuo Lin steadied his horse near the paper carton factory. His first call was to Xiao An, who he asked to bend down and become his horse. But Xiao An was a sharp child, how could he be Zuo Lin's horse. He threatened him as he pushed the other boy aside:

"Be careful with me, Zuo Lin, or I'll get San Ba to come and beat you up."

"San Ba who? said Zuo Lin. "Tomorrow I'll get my cousin to beat up San Ba!"

Zuo Lin shrank back into the wall's shadow and carried on his way, scanning the crowd for his next target. By the time he succeeded in blocking the path of factory accountant

Zhang's eight-year-old son, he had learned from experience. Using this newly accumulated wisdom, he said:

"How come you don't have anybody to play with? I'll play with you; we can play a really fun game."

The Zhang boy stopped for a while, but once he figured out that the other child just wanted to ride him in the street like a horse, he wanted nothing to do with it at all. But no matter how hard he pushed, he could not force Zuo Lin to let him go and the little boy began to cry. Many of the factory's women turned to watch them out of the window in response to the sound, leaving Zuo Lin no choice but to release him. He had ridden away only five or six metres before stopping to look around; it seemed to him as though that bustling street was truly and suddenly quite desolate.

Even though Toon Street was filled with innumerable pedestrians, together looking like a pack of horses passing before his eyes - each and every one of them qualified to become his horse - none of these people wanted to stop and let him ride them. A train rumbled past Toon Street, the world's fastest iron stallion upon which so many could ride, and it was so close, but Zuo Lin had never had the chance to mount it. He waved at the faces as they passed by in a blur within the carriages, those people in there, just like a train of horses passing by. In the pallid autumn sun, Zuo Lin felt a profound sense of loneliness.

When Zuo Lin came dejectedly to the railway bridge opening, he saw the dumpy figure of the fool Guangchun swaying from side to side as he ground away at a lock.

"Fool, what are you playing at?" said Zuo Lin.

"Don't you know that locks have got copper in them?" said the fool Guangchun. "I'm getting it out."

"Fools are fools," said Zuo Lin. "You'll spend all that energy milling out a speck of copper? That's bullshit, buying stations won't even accept it."

"I'm not taking it to a buying station," said The fool Guangchun. "I'm swapping it with the travelling salesman for some picture cards."

"You really are the biggest fool in the world," said Zuo Lin. "Can't you find this stuff back at home? I've heard your grandma was a landlord, so she's probably got gold, never mind copper."

"There's nothing in my house," said the fool Guangchun. "My grandma likes to hide stuff, I can't find anything. She hid the copper lock of her suitcase and the salesman said he'd give me fifteen cards for a lock that big. I'm going to get thirty more to complete the collection of the one hundred and eight *Outlaws of the Marsh* cards."

Zuo Lin snorted disdainfully down his nose; still trading picture cards at this age. But then, at the same time, Zuo Lin heard the clatter of hoofbeats emerging from the bridge opening, it was coming from beneath the fool Guangchun's feet. Zuo Lin's heart went wild. In this gloomy light the figure of the fool Guangchun really did give way to the impression of a horse, the fool's black plastic sandals were the modern equivalent of horseshoes, the fool's long-boned limbs the sturdy legs of a steed, the fool's round solid back a horse's hind, and the fool's unbrushed hair the bristle of a horse's mane. Zuo Lin became short of breath. His misting eyes betrayed the zealotry in his mind.

"Fool Guangchun, you're just like a horse! Fool Guangchun, you are my horse!"

And so, in a fraction of a second, the hollow became a

little prairie before his eyes, complete with a horse. Zuo Lin approached it like a cavalry leader, unable to stop himself from reaching out to pet the fool Guangchun's neck. Sleek and oily it was, just like the smooth and dense mane of the white horse of Zuo Lin's imagination. The fool Guangchun was astounded by Zuo Lin's behaviour, knocking Zuo Lin's hand away.

"Why are you touching my neck?"

Zuo Lin gazed back at the fool Guangchun, obstinately stretching out his hand to touch the fool's back. The hand communicated to him that this was the back of the broadest and safest horse in all of Toon Street. But the fool Guangchun was ticklish and laughed as he dodged, saying:

"Zuo Lin, have you gone mad? I'm not a girl, what are you touching my neck for?"

Zuo Lin looked in the direction of the pedestrians at the bridge opening and raised a silencing finger to his lips, saying:

"We're going to play a game, you're going to be a horse and I'm going to be a cavalry soldier, and you won't do badly out of it because if you do well, I'll give you a copper lock, and if you do it every day, I'll give you all of my picture cards!"

The hollow beneath the bridge witnessed Zuo Lin's promise, a truck passing over the heads of two children heard it too, but these things have neither mouth nor memory, so not a single person could provide testimony of the boy's oath. Uneasy, the fool Guangchun offered his hand to Zuo Lin to swear it. Zuo Lin hesitated for a moment before saying:

"Normally you're a fool but as soon as this stuff is involved you get clever?"

He offered his hand and solemnly locked fingers with the fool Guangchun.

The railway lumberyard was the principal site where Zuo Lin practiced his horsemanship. To get to this lumberyard from Toon Street you had to pass through three convoluted alleyways, one chemical warehouse and one pond. No one else went there. The kind of place shunned by other people was a paradise for Zuo Lin. His riding boots were his father's rubber rain boots and his horse whip was relatively easily found, too. At first he used a normal hemp rope but it looked far too clumsy, not at all like a whip, and more importantly the fool Guangchun was always grumbling that it hurt him too much, so Zuo Lin exchanged it for a twist of discarded electrical cord. With the cord as his whip, the fool Guangchun's complaints stopped, as did the satisfying cracking sound which the rope had made, much to Zuo Lin's regret.

You could also follow the railway itself to the lumberyard. It was a large area situated at the bottom of a slope and encircled by wire fencing between haphazardly placed wooden sticks. The place was quiet other than the railway workers who came to load and unload freight. There had once been a bulging-eyed tall man who watched over that place but he had already gone, maybe died or been taken back to a countryside care home. The main gate was locked but its two sides refused to unite in solidarity and so a person could be admitted through their argument if they turned their body sideways. It was in such a way that Zuo Lin and the fool Guangchun entered the yard.

The gatekeeper's cabin was empty. Through the broken window you could see a washstand and half a bedplate lying between piles of waste paper and coal cinders, the barren living quarters looked dirty, like it was concealing some sort of conspiracy within itself. Zuo Lin bore a hostility towards all gatekeepers, including that old one who had lived here. The memory had faded such that Zuo Lin didn't know when or where, but this old man had gone after him just like other people had, and had imitated the way he walked. On account of that insult, the first time they came to the yard he had convinced the fool Guangchun to shit inside the cabin. Zuo Lin felt avenged for a time but such behaviour has its negative effects. When the two of them passed by the window later, they both turned their heads and refused to look inside, knowing that one glance would reveal those two piles lying there, buzzing with flies. The worst thing about it was that the cabin could have been their very own. It was like throwing rocks at your own feet.

The autumn sun shone on the timber and weeds of the lumber yard, beside which a train occasionally sailed lithely onwards. If one of the passengers had chanced to look south-ward, they would have had the luck to witness the highlights of Zuo Lin's cavalry career; both horse and rider would have been clearly engaged in a difficult training exercise. While having another youth as a choice of steed was quite irregular, his adventures were sealed off and undisturbed. Only piles of asphalt and discarded timber served as their silent audience.

"Don't be so lazy, bend at the waist, bend," Zuo Lin was saying. "When you slant your back like this you look more like a giraffe than a horse!"

"I can't get any lower, if I go lower then I can't run," said the fool Guangchun. "You say I'm being lazy? If you don't believe me then why don't we change places and you can try it?"

"Slow down, slow down, I'm falling off," said Zuo Lin. "This isn't at all like being a cavalryman, it's like riding a donkey."

"Fast, slow, fast, slow, I'm exhausted," said the fool Guangchun. "I'm not running any more, time out, time out."

"No, I forbid it. You've only run one circle and already you're loafing around." Zuo Lin raised his electrical horse-whip high in the air, their failed session leaving him unable to control his anger and, with a crack, he heard the fool Guangchun cry out. In horror, the fool Guangchun turned his head.

"Little cripple," he said, "are you really using a whip on me? So hard?"

The fool was still standing there with his back bent like a horse but, suddenly realising something, he put Zuo Lin down and used a hand to feel his back. He could not quite touch it. He started to cry, saying:

"I'm bleeding, I'm really bleeding!"

Zuo Lin had leapt to the floor, knowing both that the fool Guangchun hated pain and that his own regret had come too late. He stood to inspect the fool's back, trying to soothe him as he did so.

"Don't worry," he said, "there's only a red mark, it cut a tiny bit of skin."

As he made his apologies, he could not have predicted that the fool would push him over, his empty eyes burning with a fiery wrath and yelling through his rage:

"I'm going to whip you!"

The fool Guangchun snatched the electrical cord from Zuo Lin's hands and tried to threaten his opponent as he dodged but, fools are fools, and act impulsively.

"I'll whip you! I'll whip you!"

Zuo Lin realised that his technique was useless as the fool Guangchun yelled, his raw strength making Zuo Lin's fear of the whip all the more terrifying and he ran back towards the lumber yard gate. And so the horse took his master's whip and the cavalryman was defeated, which would have been funny were it not for the deathly white pallor on Zuo Lin's face as his horse chased him all the way out of the gate!

Towards evening, Grandma Shaoxing burst through the door of Zuo Lin's home, dragging the fool Guangchun along behind her. They really did burst in. If she had knocked or if she had let off even a few warning curses in her irritation, Zuo Lin would have fled the approaching calamity through their window. As it was, they heard only the creaking of the door as they ate together – Grandma Shaoxing's voice came at them like a sudden clap of thunder.

"Still eating are you, Zuo Lisheng? All this rice, all this *mantou* (steamed bun), aren't you scared you'll choke?"

Zuo Lisheng's expression of vacant surprise quickly turned to anger. With one glance at Grandma Shaoxing and her grandson, he had seized his own son's hand.

"Don't move," he said. "If you run I'll break your legs!"

Although she may have added a little oil or vinegar here or there, Grandma Shaoxing's description of events was accurate and the facts were clear. He got the fool to be his horse, for which he was promised a set of *Outlaws of the*

Marsh picture cards. The fool had not received a single one and he was whipped on his back.

"Look! See what your son has done!" Grandma Shaoxing raised the fool's clothing. "Look, look, his skin's a mess. I've always thought that you were a kind and honest sort, Zuo Lisheng. I've even acted as a matchmaker for you, haven't I? How can it be that you've raised such a beast of a child? Other people bully him and now he's bullying my fool. Your ancestors' graves will emit black smoke!"

"I didn't mean to whip him," said Zuo Lin. "I didn't mean it." But before he could finish the sentence, Zuo Lisheng had slapped his son and the second half of it was swallowed.

"Kneel there," said Zuo Lisheng. "I don't want to hear a word from you. Go and fetch your picture cards and hand them over."

Zuo Lin knelt on the ground. He looked up at Grandma Shaoxing, who was still standing there, lifting the fool's clothes to reveal the welt on his back, and suddenly had the feeling that this was all so unfair. He opened his mouth to shout: "He was going to hit me..." but this sentence was swallowed just like the one before. Zuo Lisheng gave his son a second slap across the face.

"Go and get those cards, now," he said.

"You told me to kneel," said Zuo Lin.

"First go and get them," said Zuo Lisheng, "then come back and kneel. You're going to be kneeling there all night long."

Zuo Lin did not move and just kneeled upright as before. Zuo Lisheng kicked out at his son and, watching as Zuo Lin's eyes filled with tears, immediately knew what was wrong.

"You don't have any cards, do you? How can this be, all those cards your uncle gave you?" Zuo Lin turned his face to the wall and said:

"I've given them all away. The ones with Lin Chong, Lu Zhishen, Li Kui, all the good ones, I've given those to Dong Feng. Chungeng hit me and I needed Dong Feng to hit him back." Zuo Lisheng's mind anxiously raced through the situation.

"And the rest of them?"

Zuo Lin cringed, burying his face in his hands as if anticipating his father's blow and, with his voice muffled behind them, he said:

"I've given them all away, I gave all the others to Yuyong. He said he'd protect me."

Zuo Lin remembered that his father had already balled his fist, it was only the sound of the fool Guangchun's crying that came to save him. The hopeless fool's crying sounded just like the wailing of a toddler, the fright of it causing Zuo Lisheng to abandon his son to try to comfort the wailing fool. He patted the fool's head, but he shook it, shaking away Zuo Lisheng's hand and continuing his despairing, wide-mouthed wailing. Zuo Lisheng, feeling at a loss, looked up at Grandma Shaoxing.

"I'm going to beat him to death," he said. "Grandma Shaoxing, he's driving me insane. When things are this bad, how do I punish him? How do I punish myself? Tell me."

Grandma Shaoxing turned a scornful gaze to Zuo Lisheng, looking as if she had venom on the tip of her tongue – but suddenly she began to cough, a lump of phlegm coming up her throat. That ball of phlegm made her pause and, in the ensuing silence, her mind was filled with the memories of many other incidents beside this one. At once, Grandma Shaoxing began to grieve, covering her chest as she said:

"How can the lives of me and my grandson be so bitter?" She even began to cry herself.

The piercing sound, at once high and gruff, of Grandma Shaoxing and the fool's wailing resounded through the Zuo household for approximately three minutes, after which Zuo Lisheng regained his composure and proposed a sensible, fair idea. He pushed Zuo Lin down in front of the fool Guangchun, using his hand to bend his son's back.

"Guangchun, you can ride him! This is how we'll resolve this."

Zuo Lisheng used one hand to push his son, and the other to pull the fool onto the horse's back. The fool Guangchun's crying stopped, he looked like he was interested in Zuo Lisheng's proposition. He just didn't dare to rush into it. He sought Grandma Shaoxing's opinion with a glance but, finding her still sitting in the rattan chair with her eyes closed and breathing heavily, immersed in her years of sorrow, he heeded his own desire. The fool Guangchun was a little shy about the prospect of riding Zuo Lin. He said:

"The whip, Zuo Lin keeps the whip in the drawer."

"OK," said Zuo Lisheng, "I'll get it for you."

Sure enough, the electric wire was there in the drawer. Zuo Lisheng handed it over to the fool, looking at his son bent there to carry him as he did. His small, misshapen body trembled, his skinny legs along with it. He looked like a tragic semicircle. Zuo Lisheng wanted to see his son's face but wasn't able to. The boy had lowered his head into the lamplight's shadows to allow the fool to ride him.

The fool Guangchun cheered up, grinning from ear to ear as if he were filled with confidence in this role reversal.

"Uncle Zuo, can I ride him in the street?" he asked.

Zuo Lisheng looked hesitantly at Grandma Shaoxing. She opened her eyes, meeting his glance with a sharp and hard look which scared him into forcing a smile.

"Of course," he said, "of course you can ride him on the street. Zuo Lin rode you outside didn't he?"

And so, three people emerged onto Toon Street in the fading light, followed afterwards by Grandma Shaoxing. Four people, among them one cavalry soldier, one horse and two spectators who doubled as referees. The boys charged through the light of the newly lit streetlamps, bolting from east to west in a confusion of gait and speed. Pedestrians and neighbours were not at all surprised to see the younger half of the platoon but what sparked their curiosity was that Zuo Lisheng and Grandma Shaoxing were keeping the two of them company without trying to stop them.

"Grandma Shaoxing," they asked her, "why are you getting Guangchun to ride on Zuo Lin's back?"

Grandma Shaoxing, angrily thinking that their questions were not worth her while, ignored them all. Meanwhile, Zuo Lisheng was prepared to respond to them, saying:

"Children play, let children play."

Zuo Lisheng paid close attention to his son's legs and knees as he followed beside the two boys. Just as he had expected, he quickly began to hear his son's knees let out their groan. The boy did not cry but his knees did. Zuo Lisheng could not ignore that sound, splashing as it did like shards of broken glass against his heart, it was unbearable. Smiling at the fool Guangchun, Zuo Lisheng said:

"Have you vented your anger? There are still so many people and cars about, how about you get off and let him apologise again?"

But the fool Guangchun was very pleased indeed with his own horsemanship.

"No," he said. "He rode me loads of times, loads more than this."

Zuo Lisheng turned to look again at Grandma Shaoxing who did not respond to the gesture but watched the electric cable in her grandson's hand.

"You mustn't use the whip. Riding is one thing but you mustn't whip people.

"Isn't, isn't it the case that in the old society the landlords whipped the people?" she said, her voice suddenly filled with strength. Zuo Lisheng had no choice but to say:

"Carry on riding."

But Zuo Lin's knees had started to shriek. Zuo Lisheng could hear the crying and he believed that both Grandma Shaoxing and the fool Guangchun were ignoring its crackling. His knees were going to explode and nobody but him could hear the terrifying noise. They can't hear it. In that desperate situation, Zuo Lisheng still managed to think of a solution. Without offering any explanation he firmly separated the cavalryman from his horse and placed the boy on his own back.

"I'm giving you an even bigger horse to ride," said Zuo Lisheng. "Riding a big horse will be more comfortable. Quick, uncle's got you a big horse!"

Grandma Shaoxing's reaction was to try to stop the horse in its tracks. She waved her hands as she said:

"Lisheng, these are children's games, an adult isn't

allowed to get involved, where do you want me to put my face?"

She ordered her grandson to get down from his horse but he had already discovered the comfort and joy of the larger steed. He would not dismount. And so, the cavalryman and his mount ran cheering around the street, *giddyap, giddyap!* Zuo Lisheng and the fool Guangchun's cheers came high and low, both rider and horse letting out their fanatical whistle as they ran, *giddyap, giddyap!*

My cousin Zuo Lin remembers that on that night there had been a fine rain floating in the air and a few insects drifted around in the dusky lamplight. He sat on the ground, watching the fool riding proudly on his father's back. The boy looked just like a real cavalryman, whip in hand and his body upright, urging his steed ahead. He watched as the rider and the ridden were merged together, gradually disappearing into the darkness of Toon Street just like the rider had disappeared into the prairie in his dreams.

Zuo Lin cried. Zuo Lin cried and his knees cried with him, making him cry all the more miserably. And then, in the midst of his weakness and his pain, he saw the horse again. It was coming down the railroad. Not just one horse this time but a group of horses was coming towards him. They came, charging through the dark and rainy city, innumerable hooves exploding like thunder and the rain was thick with the scent of grass and horses, thick with the sound of their neighing. He felt them around him. Afterwards, he felt somebody's hands lifting him up onto the back of a horse, he didn't know whose, but they were lifting him up onto a real white Russian Don. He rode on its back, like an arrow shooting into the night sky.

IX

Cuban Knife

古巴刀

AT THE END OF THE CENTURY, intellectuals were suddenly fascinated by a Latin-American name: Che Guevara. I saw pictures of that famous man in a few magazines and newspapers; a handsome and intimidating Caucasian in a military uniform, wearing a brimless hat on his head and with a face full of whiskers. The deep, shining expression in his eyes is difficult to forget. You seldom see that kind of look nowadays and, as such, it sends a jolt through those souls who, while generally going with the flow, are yet unresigned to mediocrity. A graduate student of Western history once told me that every time she saw an image of Che Guevara, she trembled. Her undue reaction disappointed me. My feelings for that deceased and distant revolutionary are also quite distant; his image sends thoughts thronging through my mind. I guess that the photographer took that precious photograph of him somewhere in the mountains of Bolivia - he was a guerrilla fighter back in those years – but what is really interesting to me is something that exists outside the image; where is he looking, what is Guevara seeing? At first, I felt that it was an eagle because, as far as I know, the eagle is a symbol of the true revolutionary. Much later on, however, I saw an article in a newspaper which reported that Che Guevara had paid two visits to China during the sixties. The writer said that our government was engaged in the sugar trade at the time, which is the reason why so many Chinese tasted Cuban brown sugar all those years ago. I can remember it myself, the childhood image of sugar sitting in sand-dune piles in my mother's vegetable basket. I can even remember its taste. I know that this type of association with a revolutionary is quite irreverent or unjust but, for some reason, once I had read that article, I almost immediately understood the expression in Guevara's eyes. It comes from the sixties, reaching into the everlasting sky, reaching Eastern China from the other side of the planet. But what I really want to say is about that knife which Guevara is holding in the picture, using it to chop sugarcane in the fields. In junior school, my classmates and I all called that kind of knife a Cuban knife and, whether you believe it or not, I am certain that Guevara's sugarcane knife was produced in China. I can also confirm that it is the product of a factory that we knew well.

I ought to say something about that factory itself. It had never been a celebrated business in our hometown, neither then nor now. It was called the Everyday Hardware Factory at first, to the disdain of the local children, and afterwards was renamed the Knife Factory, earning itself just as much disrespect as before. It was situated on Toon Street, directly opposite the most foul and stinking public bathroom on the whole road. From time to time you would see a factory worker burst forth from their workplace, an eruption of impatience into the toilet, and then if you waited a little while you could watch them leisurely making their way back whence they had come. At school, teachers were always saying that the working class were our true leaders and so the children's aversion to the Everyday Hardware Factory came in part from the sight of those urgent bathroom visits. They suddenly knew everything there was to know about factory life. There is only one bathroom. Factory workers are like machines, machines which look after other machines. They look after the punching machine, the lathe, the miller, the planer, turning the pile of steel outside the factory into every kind of fruit knife, electrical knife, vegetable knife. Who could be interested in that kind of place? What people really want to know about are those mysterious places like an electroplating workshop, for example, where they make batteries. According to urban legend, if you fall into one of those pools you melt so that they won't even be able to scoop out your bones, you melt like ice. But nobody has heard of such a tragedy actually happening.

There is another memory about that factory - besides the Cuban knife story – which is worth sharing, and that is about its waste. People were always asking some factory worker or other whether they could take the factory's spare material out and be given the scrap for their own use. A worker told them that they could come back tomorrow, to wait outside. The children standing by the factory the next day saw iron flying out of the factory's gate partitions, pieces of metal falling onto the floor, jingling as they did. People were jubilant as they watched sheet after sheet of iron going through the puncher, cutting shapes which seemed like fresh green leaves. You can still find those leaves on the street. Along with the Cuban knife, you can still see the intimate relationship between Toon Street and that factory in the metal of people's window gates.

The factory worker to whom this intimacy is indebted is, upon closer inspection, actually the very same man whose actions created the Cuban knife story. The name of this man, the factory worker for whom all the women waited for on the day the scrap was brought out, is Chen Hui.

Chen Hui was a pale, sickly young man, the type of person who gave people the impression that he was ill just by looking at him, but nobody knew what was really wrong. The most famous youth leader on our street, San Ba, was well acquainted with Chen Hui but he didn't think there was anything wrong with him.

"The guy gets beaten up and loses blood all the time," he would say. "If you lose blood then you're gonna be pale, what's weird about that?"

Regardless, San Ba was opposed to people saying that they were friends.

"The guy's useless," San Ba would say. "He's always getting beaten up, he gives me all these knives just 'cause he's kissing my ass."

We had all seen Chen Hui turning into San Ba's home after work, pushing open the door of that foul room, bearing all kinds of fruit knives or electrical knives to serve as gifts. Sometimes, when Chen Hui brought a knife that San Ba did not like, the latter would pass it off casually to somebody else. My brother got a fruit knife from him in just that way. It had no metal plating but did have a slogan carved onto the back of the blade in cursive script:

for the people, up to the mountains and down to the villages.

The first time we saw a Cuban knife was in winter. It was a day of heavy snow upon which youngsters habitually stayed indoors. As usual, my brother and all the other boys were at San Ba's house playing novuss. As usual, Chen Hui came and overcautiously pushed open the door, his green military cap dotted with pearls of snow. As usual, nobody spared him a second glance. When Chen Hui

asked San Ba to come over to him for a moment, San Ba
did not move.

"Can't you see that I'm playing novuss," he said. "If
you've got something worthwhile just put it on the table.
Chen Hui just stood there, hesitating, and then after a few
moments they saw him stick his hand into his waistband and
carefully draw out a knife – a strange knife with a foot-long
blade, a near semi-circular edge and both of its sides already
sharpened. It sparkled with a silver-white brilliance.

"It's a Cuban knife." Chen Hui gazed expectantly at San
Ba as he spoke. "None of you know, our factory is now
producing Cuban knives."

The people in the room had never seen such a blade. It
was strange, they all thought, just like its name.

"What's a Cuban knife?" asked San Ba. "Why's it called
that?"

"I don't know," replied Chen Hui. "The factory people
call it a Cuban knife, they say it helps the Cuban revolution."

San Ba remained unconvinced. He asked Chen Hui:

"They use knives in the Cuban revolution? They go into
battle with them?"

"I heard someone saying that they're for cutting sugarcane," said Chen Hui. "Anyhow, I think it's a really good
one. I had a go at cutting iron sheets with it in the factory –
one swipe and I chopped it in two."

San Ba sneered, saying: "Cutting iron is fine but cutting
people is even better. Since it's so good, bring me a bunch of
them tomorrow, eh? All my brothers here, one per person."

An awkward expression crossed Chen Hui's face. He
avoided San Ba's eyes while he lowered his head to blow his
nose.

"They're not made in our workshop," he said. "They're from the number three workshop. They're really strict, I can't take so many."

San Ba furrowed his brow, unused to being refused by Chen Hui.

"What's the big deal with taking a few knives? I say take 'em, you take 'em. I'll sort 'em out if anybody tries to make trouble."

Chen Hui stood there watching as San Ba tossed the Cuban knife under his bed.

"I really can't take that many, the most I can get out is two or three." Looking at San Ba, he said: "You don't know, that third workshop is really strict."

San Ba waved his hand impatiently.

"Don't bother me with this crap. Do whatever's best."

Afterwards, San Ba carried on his game of novuss with my brother and the others, the bunch of them forgetting all about the knife as they played. Chen Hui came over to stand behind San Ba for a while, watching the game. The discs on the board, the kind whose destinies lay in being beaten by the cue, bounced around each of the board's four walls and corners with their melodious click. My brother also remembers that Chen Hui gave top-brand cigarettes to everybody in the room and then he was gone. The room was lively with the game, all eyes on the discs. Nobody knows when Chen Hui left.

I have already said that it was winter. By the time the first act of Chen Hui's drama began, the original snowfall had already melted and its successor was fluttering onto our city's streets. When you went outside, your eyes were filled with white. Heavy snow is rare in the south, so it was a real serendipitous gift for the children who set about turning those flakes of it which heaped onto Toon Street into snowmen. My two cousins were doing just that outside the Everyday Hardware Factory, putting them in a perfect position to witness the scene.

My cousins say that they saw Chen Hui coming out of the factory with another employee who accidentally dropped her lunchbox onto the floor. It fell right at his feet and so she turned to him and said:

"Chen Hui, pick that up for me."

Chen Hui was stunned. Standing there looking at the lunchbox on the ground, he said:

"Pick it up yourself, lazy, don't you have hands of your own?"

She used his nickname to say:

"Corpse-face, who do you think you are? You should take it as a compliment if I get you to pick something up for me!"

Chen Hui smiled and bent at the waist to retrieve the lunchbox. As he did, those nearby saw that the movement was quite stiff, as if he had a problem with his back. He changed his posture, again as if he had a problem with his spine, kneeling now to grab the box. She watched him.

"Why are you being so clumsy, corpse-face? Have you strained your back?"

He shook his head, finally lifting the lunchbox up to her while at the same time the women surrounding them heard a sound as if the cloth of his factory uniform was being ripped. They went to look at his clothes, those closest to him letting out a startled noise as they did.

There were three Cuban knives stashed in Chen Hui's waistband, three knives which had already punctured his blue overalls to reveal their clanking and glistening blades.

My cousins saw that he was surrounded by people, a bunch more running out from the office building – but he broke out from the crowd, holding the three knives up in the air as he rushed away from the group. He ran and the crowd followed. They say that Chen Hui's face was as white as the snow on the ground. A ring of keys fell from his pocket but he didn't even stop to pick them up, still holding the three knives aloft as he ran to the west side of Toon Street. The factory workers followed, shouting as they ran.

"Chen Hui," they said, "stop running, come back and explain yourself!"

Chen Hui didn't listen. He held those Cuban knives and ran like mad. Everybody on the street could see the knives so they wanted to avoid the situation, to wait and see what was going on, but eventually they too enrolled in the troop of pursuers. My cousins say that there were at least twenty people chasing Chen Hui by the end, and not one of them caught him.

Nobody could have predicted it, but they all saw it; he ran into San Ba's house. The crowd stopped outside, milling around there talking amongst themselves, some of them knocking at the door. "What has he run into San Ba's house for?" My brother was inside San Ba's house that day. He saw Chen Hui burst through the door distractedly, throwing the Cuban knives to the floor and, breathing heavily, say:

"Cuban knives. I've brought them for you."

San Ba heard the commotion outside.

"What's all this," he said. "Why's it so loud out there?"

He looked out of the window and, realising what had happened, said:

"You've been caught? You've let people catch you and then come running to my house?"

Chen Hui just stood there, not daring to look San Ba in the eye.

"Make them go away," he said. "You can make them go away."

San Ba stared at him coldly, making no reply. Then Chen Hui turned to the other people in the room with his request.

"It's you who wanted Cuban knives," he said. "I just fetched them. You guys go and make them go away."

"Such loyalty," San Ba began as he rested his cue on the board, "stealing knives and then coming running to my house. If you had killed someone, would you still have come running here?"

Chen Hui still didn't dare to look at San Ba. He turned his head to listen to the commotion outside, already louder by then - you could even make out the Northern accent of the factory's chief of security mingling with the knocking.

"Comrade San Ba," the voice called out. "Open the door. Comrade San Ba, think about the consequences!"

According to my brother, the room was tense. They all looked to San Ba who seemed as calm as ever at a glance – but even he was a little nervous. His eyes flashed over the knives on the ground and then over Chen Hui's face, his expression retaining a deceptive smile. After about five minutes of silence in the room, the noise outside becoming louder and sounding now like the police had arrived, San Ba glanced out of the window. Afterwards, he bent over and picked up the knives, straightening the three of them together and pushing them into Chen Hui's grasp.

"Take them," he said, "and get out."

Everybody in the room saw Chen Hui's expression of hopelessness. He didn't take the knives.

"They're for you," he said. "They're the knives you wanted."

My brother says that he saw a trace of a tear in the man's eye, he says that he thought Chen Hui was going to cry when he spoke.

San Ba didn't look at him.

"Open your hands, take them. Do you hear me? Give me your hands!"

They watched San Ba grip the knives under his own chin and twist Chen Hui's arm, forcing him forwards so that he could drop the knives into his hands.

"Coward," he said. "Take these and fuck off."

They watched Chen Hui standing there, dumb-founded, holding the knives. His lip was bleeding, trembling, as he turned to San Ba with wrath in his eyes. They watched Chen Hui take two steps towards the door before he turned again to San Ba, his lip still trembling but making no sound.

"What the fuck are you staring at me for?" said San Ba. "Get the fuck out, fuck off!"

And then, in an instant, something unbelievable happened. My brother says he saw fire, burning in Chen Hui's eyes, burning red hot in the middle of his white face. He let forth a moan, saying:

"San Ba, I know you."

After that, they saw Chen Hui change his grip on the

knives, grabbing two in his right hand and leaving the other
in his left.

"San Ba," he said. "Open that door. If you don't dare
even to open the door, then it's you who's the coward."

As soon as San Ba opened the door for him, Chen Hui
flew out of there like a cavalryman from the movies, madly
brandishing those knives before him. The crowd fled but
there were those within it who were too frightened to move.
They saw him roar, they saw him wielding those knives into
the crowd on either side and they didn't know which way to
dodge. They were cut down. My brother and the others in
San Ba's house watched from the windows, all of them
wanting to know what Chen Hui was actually going to do.
They watched the knives flashing in his hands with an impu-
dent air, some of them even shouting out to him in encouragement to chop, chop! Screams came from the street. My
brother says that one of the boys who had been in the crowd
fell through San Ba's window and that some of the kid's hot
blood landed on his face. Then he saw that the boy had
stretched out a hand to him, saw his other arm, saw that it
was snapped like a branch, dangling from the window frame.

The suddenness of the bloodshed threw everybody into
disorder, the Everyday Hardware Factory employees and the
police alike. They couldn't approach Chen Hui.

"Grab him, grab him," came the cry continuously but
nobody could subdue him. The crowd dispersed totally, terri-
fied by Chen Hui's madness. Those he cut down were that
boy who fell through the window, a girl who worked at the
grocery store, a peasant who sold spinach and an old man
who had difficulty walking. But then, when he dropped a
knife on the floor, something unimaginable happened. As

Chen Hui bent to retrieve the knives, he glanced up at the windows of San Ba's house. He saw San Ba, he saw that crowd of young men and he saw that they were looking at him. He picked up the knives, his nose began to twitch and then everybody heard it as the crazed Chen Hui opened his mouth and cried, wailing with his mouth as wide as a mistreated child. My brother says that the police and the security officer used that opportunity to grab his hands.

"The guy just isn't cut out for it," my brother remembers San Ba saying. "He's just an idiot posing as a hero – the truth will always out!"

It was after the last note in Chen Hui's tragedy had already been sounded that a scrawny old woman in an apron came to San Ba's door. Somebody recognised her as Chen Hui's mother. Those inside playing novuss saw that she was holding a feather duster in her hands, using it to knock at San Ba's windows. They carried on playing their novuss.

"Don't mind her," said San Ba, "she'll give you a good whack with that thing, even if it's only made of feathers."

They paid no attention to her. Somebody got up and drew the curtains, and before long they heard the sound of her crying.

"Let her cry," said San Ba, "ignore her. If we let her in there'll be trouble."

They carried on playing novuss, the pieces tapping away on the board. Before long, Chen Hui's mother was no longer tapping on the window, and the sound of her crying gradually floated westward. It was quiet once more. San Ba stood up to open the windows, looking out into the street.

"Chen Hui's definitely in cuffs right now," he said.

The boys around him joined a chorus of agreement.

"D'you think he got the chance to escape?"

"He's cuffed."

Afterwards, they heard San Ba suddenly burst out laughing.

"Have a look, look what I've got."

He turned around, a smile spreading suddenly on his face, and they all saw that he was holding a feather duster.

Cuban knives became fashionable after the Chen Hui incident. That winter, all anybody could talk about was Chen Hui and, naturally, they also talked about those knives. Eventually, even women and children came to know all about the ferocious Cuban knife. According to rumour, the Everyday Hardware Factory held a meeting after the affair where the police went to tell them not to remove those knives from the factory. I don't know how they ended up finding a route out of there and I don't know who decided to follow in Chen Hui's footsteps either, but there was a fight between a bunch of gangsters in a coal yard in '78 where the police found that the weapons responsible were Cuban knives. But I'm sure that this is something that everybody on Toon Street has heard about anyway. What nobody has heard before is what I was talking about earlier, about that Latin American man Che Guevara.

I don't mean to tell Che Guevara's story; his tale doesn't belong to me. Even though that outstanding revolutionary once held one of our knives in his hands, I know that he still has no real relationship with us, nor do I have any reason to invent one.

It is a strange experience, making a long-ago murdered

revolutionary into an intimate friend, but I love his expression and I love his cap, and through this love I have invented some absurd fantasy in his image. I imagine the hot dry season of Cuba, sugar cane stretching as far as the eye can see. I imagine Che Guevara standing in one of them, chopping away with that familiar knife. In this scene, his high-born mother becomes an ordinary peasant woman. She comes from the hillock, carrying a basin of water from a thatched cottage. She waits for her son to return home from the fields. I have never seen a photograph of her, so in my mind that Latin American woman's face is just like my own mother's. I see her face clearly, leaning on the door as she waits for her son. She looks just like my mother in the seventies, waiting for my brother to come home in the dead of night.

And then I see her turn around and go into her cottage. When she comes out again, she is holding a feather duster.

X

The Madonna Business

玛多娜生意

ONE

I WAS IN BUSINESS too back then.

Pang De and I had partnered together to open the Iris Marketing Agency, which enjoyed a flourishing popularity over the course of five entire months. Pang De packed a bunch of prospective clients into our office every day - so much so, in fact, that the coffee machine broke twice and we used up a load of those boxes of disposable cups. Later, though, I found out that there were never actually any contracts. Those people had just come to chat about art with Pang De. There was this rock and roller who got drunk on beer and started pissing in all our plant pots – pinching his organ between his fingers and yelling: *"Come on! Come on!"*. The azaleas, philodendrons and money trees knew nothing about it but they shrivelled up after a few days all the same.

I ought to introduce Pang De. He is my friend, an amateur poet, a fancier of music and art, and generally acknowledged as the greatest artistic talent among our friends. But then he was the manager of our office. If artistic talent doesn't make any money, then what's the use? Anybody could imagine my panic during the final stages of that five-month disaster. My admiration for Pang De had soured into aversion. I had taken to mocking his incompetence and sneered at everything that he loved. I spoke about the rottenness of poetry, the uselessness of music, I even attacked his most beloved artist - Picasso. I said that he was nothing more than a sex obsessive. Pang De's rejoinder was reasonable, quite logical really.

He said: "I ask you, does losing a little money entitle you to slander the arts?"

After that I listened to him while he coolly defended himself.

"It's all the fault of this superstar from Hong Kong who failed to keep their appointment"

You just can't rely on a friend's introduction for cooperation in business. One of them was a swindler and after that we had talks with this furniture dealer who turned out to be totally illiterate. Somehow or other we came to the matter of the company name, to which he grumbled about our blind compliance with a certain painter when she had suggested we use that unlucky moniker 'Iris'.

"An iris flower blooms only briefly, you know? When Van Gogh painted an iris he went crazy, you know? It's fate, the iris's curse has been fulfilled and now you've all forced me into madness."

Seeing as he had brought that old matter up, I said:

"I'd originally wanted to call it Southern Prairie, remember?" To which he replied vociferously:

"Southern, Prairie, what an open and pleasant name! You were the one who opposed it."

In those days, Pang De also insisted on renting the office at the Pacific Ocean Hotel, complete with staff. His Santana would haunt that hotel every day, with him emerging from it in his western suit and leather shoes.

"Don't worry," he said, in an attempt to calm our team, "the tree's final apple is the reddest and the sweetest."

Then somebody told me that it was his girlfriend Peach's birthday, and that he had given her seventy-seven roses. This caused me a great deal of annoyance. He was going to completely squander the remainder of our accounts with his romantic pursuits. So, again, I gave him a call to denounce his actions. Just as before, Pang De and I fell out. The tone of his voice over the phone had become arrogant and sharp.

"If you're counting your pennies like that, you can just withdraw them. I really don't care." After this malicious outburst he became silent and suddenly revealed his hand. It was incredible. He asked me, quietly:

"Madonna, you know Madonna? I'm telling you, Madonna is coming, we'll have a huge deal, any day now."

I went to meet Pang De in the Pacific Hotel coffee shop.

He was sitting opposite a young woman who was a stranger to me, drinking coffee, talking, shrugging his shoulders. He seemed so elegant and in higher spirits than ever when he was sitting there with that woman, doing this shoulder-shrugging action that he did all the time. As I walked over, he seemed to have forgotten his earlier annoyance and gave me a very generous introduction to the woman beside him.

"Jian Mali from Shenzhen, our partner in the Madonna business." Having said that, seeing my doubtful expression, he elbowed me in the side and lowered his voice to say: "She's Mr Jian's niece."

I certainly knew who that was. The so-called godfather of the marketing agency, the big shot, a legendary success who had traversed legitimate, illegitimate and even governmental routes with expertise. Yet, I instinctively distrusted the validity of this description; Pang De tends to exaggeration and confusion in his stories, all contributing to my growing feeling of suspicion, my desire to safeguard against the intentions of this woman. I remember very clearly that

Mali did not stand to greet me, apparently volleying my suspicion right back. She frowned and lazily stretched out her hand for me to take in an expression of obvious charity. She wiped the dregs of coffee from her lips with a napkin, rolled it into a ball and tossed it into the ashtray, saying indignantly:

"What's this coffee called?" With a glance at the distant waiter she added, magnanimously: "A place makes whatever kind of coffee suits it, I'll let it slide. When I take you to the Sheraton, you'll see their Lanshan coffee is pretty good."

There's a fashion, high-class and mysterious, for wearing a leather skirt with ankle boots and a white shirt. Her skin was a little dark and her face rather square – beauty was totally out of the question – but there was something about her. When she looked at Pang De, her eyes were vibrant, and when she smiled at him it was charming, shy, as if she was still a little girl. When she occasionally shot a glance in my direction, however, her expression was totally different. I found only something proud and unfeeling in her gaze towards me, which I believe was quite deliberate on her part. She wanted me to know that she didn't trust me.

I didn't really participate in their discussion. They fervently discussed Madonna; her voice, her staging, her figure, the colour of her hair. They even talked about her new husband, an English director who had most recently produced some gangster movie which was apparently full of romance and murder. I impatiently enquired about the particulars of Madonna's tour but Pang De put a stop to it, saying that we didn't have the qualifications to be discussing these details yet and, as to whether or not Iris would receive this contract, we would still have to wait for Madonna to come to Shenzhen to talk - and that was all up to Mr Jian. It sounded like a reasonable response. I asked Jian Mali:

"Is Mr Jian your father's older or younger brother?"

She pursed her lips and turned a questioning glance in the direction of Pang De, who shrugged his shoulders as usual. She suddenly fixed me with a severe expression.

"Guess!"

I couldn't see any weakness in her eyes but instead a hint of childish mischief. I did the Pang De shrug.

"How could I guess?"

She suddenly let out a grim laugh.

"Actually, you did guess."

Then, she fished out some lipstick from her purse and began to fix up her lips, asking me:

Mr Lu, you've heard of Madonna?"

I said that I knew of her but I had forgotten what she sings. She flashed me a sidelong glance and then suddenly a splendid smile.

"I know what you men like most, *Like a Virgin*. D'you like it?"

After that, in spite of mounting expectations, the business with Madonna was left unsettled. Fortunately, nobody insisted on pressing the issue, and apart from the expense of Pang De accompanying Jian Mali on a trip to Huangshan and Hangzhou, Iris didn't suffer any financial damage. Was Jian Mali a charlatan? For a while that question became our greatest mystery and a difficult one to investigate, at that.

Among our group of friends there was somebody in Shanghai who met with Mr Jian and was fortunate enough to exchange a few words with him. Naturally, they asked about the business with Madonna. Mr Jian's reply confirmed that it was true but just acting as an intermediary, nothing more. They were unable to discuss any kind of advance payment on a production contract and the business finally fell through. When asked about Jian Mali, Mr Jian denied it flatly, saying that he had never had a niece. Everybody had heard something of Mr Jian's romantic life - he always moved in a cloud of pretty girls - but he denied that any of them were his niece. That friend of ours was forced to come up with an excuse; it must just have been a coincidence. The surname 'Jian' is not common but that young woman just happened to share it.

Iris quickly wilted and the office closed its doors. Pang De was furious for many days, dejected for a spell and finally wandered along to the former office, staring blankly at a picture album on his desk while holding a box cutter in his hands. Somebody noted that the image was not unlike Van Gogh cutting off his own ear and so warned him:

"Pang De, don't take things too hard, businesses open and close all the time. If you cut off your ear how will you pick up girls? If you chop up your ears, how are you going to listen to music?"

"Don't disturb me," he said. "I've already left my madness behind. Now, I'm merely in the position of coming to terms with betrayal and grief."

Fortunately, Pang De finally changed his grief into strength and used the utility knife to carve the following four characters into his desk: *Lofty Aspirations Went Unrealised.* It was a slow and difficult task because he wrote it in ancient script. After that, he put the knife in the bin and swaggered off.

Then there was a period of time in which Pang De

vanished without a trace. Nobody could find him, including his girlfriend Peach. Pang De had described to us his plan for a better life - the most unsurpassably astonishing component being that he was going to go to Kumbum monastery in Qinghai to become a monk – but these enumerations certainly never contained the strategy to 'go missing'. Some people guessed he had gone to the United States, as that had been a dream of his for many years. But Peach told us that Pang De's visa had been rejected by the American embassy, despite the fact that it was only to go to a Madonna concert in Las Vegas. He also had this plan to study abroad at Harvard but that had been nothing more than a brief and empty fantasy.

Peach was a lute teacher at the Children's Palace, a public facility for extra-curricular activities. She had a reputation for being a virtuous woman with a striking resemblance to the singer Teresa Teng. Before Pang De's maniacal, three-year-long pursuit of her, he would have been an obscure choice of lover. Peach's parents resented Pang De's boasting and unreliability, and had opposed the match all along. By the time she had finally persuaded her parents and they were prepared to discuss marrying her off, Pang De had vanished. We all sympathised with Peach's situation. Her life was accustomed to two things: Pang De's love, and teaching children how to play the lute. Without Pang De, the children and the lute became more expendable; Peach's life had thoroughly lost its balance. She became wan and sallow, complaining miserably, from which we learned that she blamed us, Pang De's friends, for his disappearance. It was us that had pulled him into our ship of brigands, and when the ship of brigands sank, nobody had looked out for him. Crying her heart out, Peach instructed everybody to communicate her ultimatum to Pang De. If he did not return before International Children's Day, she would take her lute and jump from the tower of the Children's Palace. These may have seemed like empty words but Peach was overcome with tears when she told us, not at all like a person making idle threats. Looking at the image of this educated, well balanced, lovely woman, we at once sank into the depths of despair. Everybody was heartbroken and sighed with the sorrow of love's painful changeability. Everyone said that their love was a jar of honey which, once overturned, would congeal into a sharpened blade to pierce us all.

And so the responsibility of finding Pang De became a matter of life or death, and also the responsibility of our group of friends. Our friend from a securities company was the first to find a clue. It was one of those pictures in which an event photographer had haphazardly flashed images all over the place. The background lighting was in dazzling disorder, so the whole thing was a little vague, but you could still make out the high-spirited face of Pang De within it. He was leaning on a foreign woman by his side, silver-haired and red-lipped, the light of romance radiating all around. We cried out in shock.

"Madonna, it's Madonna!"

No. Clearly, we must have all simply mistaken her for Madonna. Could Pang De really have gone to America? So soon? Had he really met Madonna?

We soon regained our composure. It was impossible. On closer inspection, we realised that Madonna could not have been the real one, she must have been an impersonator, a double and nothing more. Looking carefully at the photograph, we could see a banner with the slogan from some company's IPO. The artificial Madonna beside Pang De exuded a vacant but bewitching expression; she could easily have been mistaken for the real thing. But, by carefully screening her features, we realised that she was Chinese. Who was she? People gave the names of popular singers. As for me, I soon made the connection to Jian Mali. It was just the impression of her, the square shape of her face, acting as Madonna. How could her face have been so long like that? The bridge of the nose, the shape of the eye, could that have been makeup?

News later confirmed my intuition. That Madonna was known as Shekou Madonna, and the woman known as Shekou Madonna was really Jian Mali. Our duty to find Pang De had evolved into a secret investigation into this girl.

The truth quickly came to light. Jian Mali's background was not as mysterious as Pang De had suggested but was also not as simple as we had imagined. Originally, she was an actress in a song and dance troupe in a small town in eastern Sichuan. Immediately after that she had gone south to Shenzhen where she became a dancer specialising in evening entertainment. Not long afterwards, the dance company disbanded, the friends went their separate ways and only she remained, studying singing. There were plenty in Shenzhen who enjoyed hanging around the theatre to see her wild singing and dancing, saying that her singing was so-so, often lip-syncing, but her image was hard to forget; electrifyingly provocative, incomparably sexy. Her stage name, Shekou Madonna, was just right - she even lived in Shekou. Somebody who knew about her personal life said Jian Mali was once kept as a mistress by a businessman from Hong Kong.

On one occasion – they didn't know why – she took off her high heels to chase and beat the businessman from the elevator to the lobby and into the parking lot of their apartment building. Neighbours saw her use the shoes to smash a hole in the window of his car, after which she walked barefoot back to the apartment, carrying the shoes in her hand and saying to her neighbour:

"Well this is fun."

After that she had a special nickname in the building; 'Fun'. There were also people who had seen her on TV. She entered many talent shows, had a few walk-on parts on TV shows, and was even on a Korean beauty cream commercial. There was all sorts of news relating to Jian Mali but our greatest concern was with her current situation. It was clear where she was now but nobody dared to tell Peach.

We heard that Jian Mali and Pang De were already living together in Shenzhen.

TWO

Towards the end of May, Peach's parents went to Shenzhen with Pang De's older brother and his wife to force him to return.

I don't know why, but Pang De did come back and, to our amazement, did so like a conquering general. He invited all of us together. Our meeting place was not at the Pacific Ocean Hotel like before but in a Sheraton. We were drinking champagne and eating steak which was all clearly very expensive. Peach was also there and said very little, merely holding sadly onto Pang De's hand, informing us of the hardship of losing love and finding it again. He was wearing an odd Western-style black suit with a white trim. We expressed interest in his suit but he didn't find it worthwhile, saying:

"You are all accustomed to wearing fake goods, so what you're feeling is just a naïve expression of excitement due to ignorance, you know? Armani's new style always pushes the boundaries."

We all asked what he meant by 'pushing the boundaries' but he said he couldn't be bothered to explain, shrugged his shoulders and gave us his new business cards. The business was called Tropical Storm Talent Agency. He was holding three roles simultaneously: legal, chair and CEO. Some of our friends said sarcastically:

"Pang De, were those the only duties you undertook in Shenzhen? Nothing more than that?"

But Pang De didn't mind and said, laughing at himself:

"I didn't write the other duties on my business card."

Peach's face abruptly changed colour at hearing these implications, so nobody had the heart to make fun of him any longer. In any event, the danger of Children's Day had already passed, so their reunification was a good thing. At least, it spared us friends from worry.

At first nobody was aware that Jian Mali had also returned, either following or accompanying Pang De. He would later deny that he knew she had come back but we were unable to confirm whether that was a lie. When we reflected on that happy meeting at the Sheraton however, we remembered that when Peach went to the bathroom, we saw that someone had used red lipstick to draw a big red cross on the skirt of her white *cheongsam*.

The day was the fifth of June. Rumour had it that

Peach's diplomatic approach to the situation had already faltered but she was still teaching at the Children's Palace. The children in her lute class said that golden-haired Auntie Madonna was waiting for Ms Peach at school, after which Uncle Pang De also came along. The children could hear Uncle Pang De and Auntie Madonna arguing outside the classroom. They followed Ms Peach out to meet them. By that time, Uncle Pang De had already left. It was in this way that the day's lute class came to its hasty conclusion. The children saw Ms Peach and Auntie Madonna talking together, at first on the lawn, but then Ms Peach carried her lute along to the tower with Auntie Madonna following along behind her.

They stood together at the top of the tower where a brightly coloured Young Pioneers of China flag blew in the wind. They stood beneath that flag as if in a lovers' meeting. Two figures, one black, one blue. The children couldn't hear what was being said at the top of the tower, they could only see the long confrontation of black and blue. Suddenly, they heard Auntie Madonna's shrill voice:

"Jump then, you jump and I'll jump with you!"

The children saw their teacher holding onto the railing and weeping, looking like she really was in danger of jumping. A clever child called the other teachers. The calligraphy master, who some said had been in love with Peach all along, came first. He ran directly to the tower, followed shortly by the headmistress Mrs Yan who didn't dare to ascend the tower but, with her face deathly white and her lips trembling, shouted questions up to the roof.

"Young woman, where did you come from?"

Madonna answered that she had come from the planet

earth. Mrs Yan stamped her feet and addressed Peach with stern criticism:

"This is the Children's Palace! Look at that banner above your head! Don't let romance muddle your brain - the children can all see you! In front of the children's faces, beneath the flag of our academy, how can you dare? Get down at once!"

The whole time while Peach was being helped down by the calligraphy master, she used her lute case to cover her face - showing that she didn't want the children to see her crumbling apart. But the lute case could not conceal the truth of her shaking body. Her trembling didn't cease when she stopped to address the children.

"I'm sorry, I'm sorry, I'm too weak, not fit to be your teacher."

A little girl grabbed hold of Ms Peach and, making it clear what she felt in her heart, spat at Madonna.

"You're not Madonna, you're a devil!"

The people of the Children's Palace all looked at Auntie Madonna. She was dressed all in black, adorned with two huge shell earrings and with a ring of multi-coloured cloth around her ankle from which dangled a red bell. They saw her crease her brow and use a napkin to wipe away the girl's spit. She lifted her face again, and a tolerant smile appeared on her scarlet lips.

"You're young, you don't understand Madonna." She used a finger to stroke the girl's face. "Sometimes Madonna is a goddess, sometimes she's a devil."

THREE

This was how Jian Mali became a dark legend.

That event in June caused us all to lose hope with Pang De, to the extent that we didn't even know why he'd bothered to return - to reconcile with Peach or to break things off with her. Ultimately, he just couldn't make up his mind. He wanted Peach but he also wanted Jian Mali. Some of his remaining friends had frank words with him, warning him that if Jian Mali could be so callous with Peach, she could be the same way with him in the future. Pang De defended her.

"You don't understand her," he said. "She's really very kindhearted.

Someone caustically raised the question: "Is she as kindhearted as a stone or a wolf?

"As all of us," he said, continuing: "When we're together, you don't know how good she can be."

This could well have been the case, love can do that. Nobody refuted him, so he became more spirited, saying:

"You all guess, how many homeless cats has she adopted?" Nobody paid any attention, so he raised his hand as he answered himself, saying: "Five cats, she took in five homeless cats, one called Bai Ma, another called Hua Ma; they sleep with us."

Then he looked at us all expectantly, waiting for somebody to ask what the names meant. When nobody did, he took it upon himself to explain anyway.

"Bai Ma is a white cat, standing for the pure Madonna; and Hua Ma is a tabby cat, for the Madonna in bloom, get it?" Seeing that his friends were full of ridicule he adjusted his tie and said: "I know that you are all biased against her, you don't understand love. Love, it takes over, I'm telling you, it's love that drove her crazy."

Pang De remained in our group of friends. One might say that when under pressure one needs to make a choice, maybe he finally woke up to danger, maybe some of his love for Peach remained, or maybe it was merely some kind of fear, a fear of the threat of Peach's suicide. In any case, he and Peach got married. That day, Peach's appearance, including every frown and smile, all strikingly resembled our beloved Teresa Teng. Somebody, gazing at the bride's radiant face, suddenly let out a sigh, saying, after all, it happened on our turf. See, Teresa Teng has defeated Madonna!

And so, we had persuaded Pang De to stay. But for many of us this meant that we had persuaded a nuisance to remain in our lives. Pang De's Tropical Storm Company was still going, he had left Jian Mali, which meant that he had left Madonna, and in leaving Madonna, he had sunk himself into an unprecedented state of confusion.

He and Peach lived near the grounds of a school for deaf-mutes. One day, passing by that school, he saw two pretty, deaf-mute girls having a heated argument in sign language at the school gates, which inspired him with the queer idea to organise a televised debate tournament for deaf-mutes. I must admit, there wasn't anyone left in our group of friends who was willing to go into business with Pang De but there were still some who were willing to praise his originality.

He received their encouragement and began to busy himself with his new endeavour. The deaf-mute school, for its part, was interested in popularising its brand but the television station was reluctant to commit. They said that he could pre-record an episode, then they would review the programme and get back to him. The key to it all was to find a commercial sponsor who wanted to support a deaf debate platform which was not an easy task. In that period, we repeatedly received phone calls from Pang De and what I remember most from them was that his voice was full of enthusiasm, like a manifesto, and also like a threat.

"It will cause a sensation."

But the commercial benefits did not flow, and the social benefit of the endeavour could not be calculated.

"It will cause a sensation," he said. "The time will come when you regret this!"

Then only Peach remained close to Pang De, promoting his ideas everywhere. We did not know Mr Hao, a man in the marble business, but we heard that he was the father of one of Peach's lute students. Pang De signed a sponsorship deal with him; spoils won by the lute, or rather by Peach's lute in particular. There was a period in which Pang De was always taking Peach to dinner parties at Mr Hao's house, or perhaps you could say that it was Peach who was always taking Pang De along with her lute. After they had eaten, she would play a rendition of *River on a Spring Night* for the guests. We all knew that was the piece that she was the most skilful at performing.

On the eve of the TV recording, many of us received Pang De's invitation to the broadcast centre to witness the splendid beginning of his endeavour. He was running around in circles, too busy to greet us, so we were only hurriedly introduced to Mr Hao - a stout, dusky man from Fujian with an honest smile but revealing a certain shrewdness in his eyes. Peach was by his side, for some reason looking anxious rather than excited.

The spotlight fell on the deaf-mute children. They were debating a topic concerning love and mercy, which I believe was Pang De's idea. According to the children themselves, this was a difficult task and there was indeed one pretty, deaf-mute girl who forgot her lines and instead looked like she wanted to cry. Another boy, however, was in a fierce mood and launched an attack on his opponent with a cyclone of sign language. I asked the people beside me what he was saying, and it turns out he was accusing his opponent of being unfit to discuss love and mercy, since yesterday evening he had forced his opponent to drink a cup of urine. Suddenly, that boy turned red in the face, lifted his fingers in the shape of a gun and pretended to pull the trigger, opening fire on his opponent. Below there was an uproar - people just couldn't stop laughing. I could make out the indistinct sound of Pang De's voice by the camera yelling:

"Debate teams, stop! Stop! Cut! Cut!"

Peach and Mr Hao were still sitting quietly together, unaffected by the chaos around them. Their legs were together but that was of no great importance. Then I happened to see their hands. Even though she pulled her hand away quickly, I believe it was no fantasy of mine that I saw him holding it. Something was definitely going on between Peach and Mr Hao. I can't say what had happened between Peach and Pang De. Had she betrayed him so quickly? Had she betrayed Pang De for Pang De's own sake? Once again, their romance had thrown me into uncertainty.

Pang De's deaf-mute debate tournament was called to a halt. It had something to do with the department thinking that the show's orientation was unclear, that it touched upon a marginalised group without a palpably positive significance. He wrote lengthy appeals and rushed about between departments but in the end had no choice but to accept that his labour had come to nothing. After that he developed a hernia and had to go to hospital. When we went to visit him, he exhaustedly summarised his wins and losses.

"I was not born to have dealings with bureaucrats, I am suited to making music," he said. "Have you all heard? Mariah Carey is coming to Hong Kong!" Nobody said anything. His eyes began to light up as he went on. "I'm preparing to fly to Hong Kong to meet with her talent manager. I have a classmate in New York who knows the guy."

We saw his expression, waited for him to speak, and sure enough his voice had adopted that mysterious tone of his.

"Her manager is really interested in Chinese cities, it's a great opportunity. Are you all interested?"

So, we left him in his ward earlier than we had anticipated. We ran into Peach in the hallway outside, drowsily carrying her lute, telling us that she had just been to have one of the strings changed. We asked her whether she intended to go to Hong Kong with Pang De, to which she responded with a sad smile.

"To Hong Kong? I can't afford a ticket. It's only me who's making any money in the house." She suddenly plucked an ear-piercing high note on one of the lute's strings and said: "I'm now doing private house visits, I've become a personal tutor!"

FOUR

There was a lot of snow that winter.

On one of these snowy evenings Pang De unexpectedly rang my doorbell. Certainly, I thought, it's about time for him to come up with some scheme. He was wearing a wool sweater and pyjama bottoms, all covered in snow. He raised his hands and I saw that he was carrying a bottle of cooking wine.

"See, all the wine at my house is gone," he said. "There's nowhere to get it right now, lend me a bottle."

His eyes were shattered and he was already staggering as he walked. I brought him into the room, he was very grateful and unexpectedly kissed me on the cheek, his breath stinking of alcohol.

"Friends are still good," he said. "There is only friendship, friendship is eternal."

I could already guess what had happened. Peach had gone to Mr Hao's house to tutor his daughter and had been making some unexpected music. Pang De and Peach had been separated for many days - our group of friends had already heard about it. Nobody had anticipated things would play out like this, for Pang De to do the right thing in the nick of time, and for Peach to change her mind shortly afterwards. We heard that Mr Hao's wife once went to the Children's Palace, I don't know why, and finally ended up on top of the tower. Peach followed the woman and they stood up there, side by side, with Peach saying:

"You decide whether or not you want to jump. If you want to jump, just count one, two, three, and I'll jump with you."

This really sounded like a rumour, Peach could not have morphed into Jian Mali so quickly. Nobody dared to trust it but there was somebody who knew the school's painting master and, according to his mumbling, stilted testimony, there seemed to be some truth in it.

I didn't know how to talk sense into him. We sat drinking. He didn't speak and, pointing to his throat, with his hands covering his chest, he indicated that his voice was hoarse and that he was heartbroken. I feared that he wanted to talk about his marital crises with me, to sound me out on some plan.

"You've had too much to drink, you're not yourself, let's talk about poetry and music, Picasso even.

He sized me up with his eyes flashing, detecting my fear, and suddenly let out a sharp, cold laugh.

"Poetry, it's bullshit. Music, also bullshit." He paused for a second, let out a hiccup and, from his hoarse throat, declared:

"Who even is Picasso? He's nothing more than an art whore."

I almost wanted to laugh but didn't have the heart to. I interjected:

"Madonna? Mariah Carey? Who are they?"

He thought for a moment, not wanting to rush into denouncing his former idol, but firmly shook his head.

"I don't listen to them now; one is too commercial, the other too superficial. As he spoke, he produced a CD out of the pocket of his sweater.

"Take this and listen to it, stunning, stunning. Now I listen to this every day. Listen to it, it'll improve your mood."

It was a black-cased imported CD, a silvery skull with

garish red lips on the cover. I didn't recognise the line of foreign writing, so Pang De gave them an introduction. Skull and Rose, an underground Manhattan rock group. Curiously, I put the CD into my stereo player. It sounded like a bunch of moaning, followed by glass breaking and a car speeding, and then a tractor, along with the sound of a bulldozer, then all kinds of electrical instruments came pouring in, intermingled with the frantic screeches of a woman's voice. It was the dead of night, so I hurriedly popped the CD out and asked him:

"Who gave you this CD? It's a complete racket."

His face showed that mysterious expression which I knew so well.

"Guess." I don't guess, as a rule. He said: "It was Jian Mali who gave it to me. She's in New York."

"You know who that female singer is?" he asked again. I shook my head.

"You can't make it out? It's Jian Mali! The band, keyboardist, guitar, bass, drummer, they're not white - they're black people! They perform in Hell's Kitchen, have you heard of Hell's Kitchen? Jian Mali isn't a dancer, she's a rocker, a success!"

I knew that Jian Mali had gone to New York. I thought that she had gone to find Madonna, and expected that she might have found work in a Chinese restaurant or laundry for the time being. While Pang De spoke of Jian Mali's success, I instinctively felt suspicious. However, he wouldn't allow me any doubt. He clenched his fist and beat it on his thigh.

"I was wrong about her. I said just give me five years, I can turn you into an international superstar; none of you believed me." He became emotional as he spoke, holding his head and saying: "I was wrong about her, and I wronged myself, I don't blame you all, I blame my own kidnapping."

I was taken aback. "Who kidnapped you?"

He looked at me angrily, and suddenly howled: "Morality! And you hypocritical friends! You took advantage of my kindheartedness!"

He began to demonstrate his skill at holding a one-man question-and-answer session.

"What is kindheartedness, do you know?" he said. "I'll tell you, kindheartedness, it's the biggest and foulest moral bullshit!

Snow floated outside the window. I imagined that, at this moment, snow was also falling on the streets of New York, and tried to picture what Jian Mali might be doing right now. But in my head was just a void. My impression of Jian Mali had already become fuzzy, so what appeared instead was the image of Madonna herself, singing and dancing, loud and suffocating, but also with something bewitching and alluring lying with her in that space as well. It was truly strange, a girl from eastern Sichuan, holding this position, this impression of Madonna, within my memory.

On that snowy night Pang De stayed over at my house. He was seriously drunk and threw up twice in the bathroom. The first time he vomited he was still clear-headed and divulged to me his life plan. He said that he was waiting for Jian Mali's green card and when she got it he could go to America. The second time was worse. He grabbed onto the toilet bowl, tears falling from his eyes. He held the toilet and wept, babbling nonsense. He said he wanted to swim to America through the toilet, if he could do that, Jian Mali would be waiting for him by the sewer's exit.

FIVE

It looked like Pang De's path from the country was as distant as the Silk Road. Jian Mali's green card was a long time coming and he couldn't wait. So a travel agent friend of his planned a long and strange route for him. First, he would go to Yunnan, then from Yunnan to Vietnam, then from Vietnam to Australia. Then, according to his original plan, he would cross the Pacific Ocean. The destination had not changed, it was still the USA.

The majority of our friends had received pictures of Pang De at the gates of the Sydney Opera House - a group photo before an advertisement for Karajan's performance. He said that he had heard Karajan's concert, and that it was incomparably stunning. Then he had heard Wagner's opera *Der Ring des Nibelungen*, which was inevitably even more stunning. This certainly aroused people's envy, it's just a pity we can't get to know the truth. We had a friend in Sydney. We received letters from him at first, for the most part trifles about finding a job and an apartment, but soon lost track of him. Everybody thought he had found a way of getting to the US but later we found out that Pang De wasn't able to go to America, whether through his own mistakes or because Jian Mali had experienced some misfortune over there, we don't know. He concealed the truth and moved to New Zealand where he went to pick grapes at a winery.

Nobody anticipated this move to New Zealand, or that he would stay picking grapes for that many years. In the end, it was grapes that changed his life. Approximately five summers later, we heard the news one by one. Pang De was back, with a New Zealand passport in his pocket. He had come back in the name of some manager of a winery in New Zealand, with the intention of opening up the market. In passing, he invited all of us to his wine-tasting event.

After five years, Pang De was as impressive as ever, wearing smart clothes. We had imagined that the changes in his life would have left behind some changes on his face, but the stretching of his white, skin-tight Western trousers across his belly betrayed only that he had put on a little weight. He showed us several types of grape, speaking without pause about the tannins, the sweetness, the fruity aroma, Pinot Noir, these kinds of words which none of us understood. The only person he paid attention to throughout the tasting was a white man with earrings, about forty years old and occupied mostly with greeting foreigners but who would often shoot meaningful, secretive glances at Pang De. We all saw there was an intimate relationship between that man and Pang De, so we quietly asked him about it. Pang De said:

"That's Jack, a great master winemaker." Pang De suddenly smiled, and the smile was a little bashful. Everybody looked at him and it was unclear what he was smiling at. Afterwards, we all heard him lower his voice and say: "Fuck, I'm a bunch of Syrah grapes being turned into a glass of Chardonnay!"

None of us knew anything about wine, nor understood this obscure but sincere announcement. Pang De had laid aside his American dream but I remembered it well. I remembered that oath he had made on a snowy night and so I couldn't help but remind him about it.

"In all these years, after all is said and done, did you or did you not ever go to New York? Did you get to see Jian Mali?" He heaved a sigh.

"I went, I saw her, by that time she was already the mother of two children."

I asked who she had married, to which he replied, nobody. She had one girl, who was half white, and one boy, who was half black. I was speechless, and asked:

"How about now, is she waiting for you?"

He shrugged his shoulders, that action that was so typical of him. I probed further.

"How come you're still single, are you still waiting for her?"

He let out a fleeting, exaggerated laugh, I didn't know whether it was contempt for my silly question or a sign of sadness.

"Do you know who I'm waiting for?"

He quickly shifted into a crafty expression, shooting a glance at the distant figure of Jack, and snapped his fingers.

"I'll tell you, Jack and I are waiting for Li Ka-shing. Li Ka-shing has already bought our neighbouring winery, so we are waiting for him to buy ours." He swirled his wine cup in his hands. "You've seen our wine, the body, the fruity fragrance!" Pang De went on. "It's all Pinot Noir, Marlboro, we're no worse than them!

So, Pang De and Jian Mali were still separated by the Pacific Ocean. They were still friends, however, and it was two years ago in spring when I suddenly received a telephone call from Pang De saying that Mali wanted to bring her children back to visit her family and that she was going to stay in our city. He wanted us friends to receive her. Frankly speaking, everybody wanted to see the legendary Jian Mali and how she looked as a mother, so we all readily assented. To ensure that she remembered us, and to focus attention on that story of shattered love, we made arrangements to meet her at the Pacific Ocean Hotel.

We invited Jian Mali to eat with us. She came along in a leisurely fashion, bringing her two mixed-race children along with her. She wore a white *cheongsam* inlaid with a blue border. Her hair had been restored to black and gathered up into a classic bun. Her face was thickly covered with foundation and her lipstick was very heavy. Time's mark had been prudently erased from her - she looked like a girl from a tobacco ad from the thirties. Some frankly expressed their feelings, and she smiled dryly, saying:

"My appearance is really ordinary, this retro style is fashionable in New York right now."

I brought some wine along with me from Pang De's winery. She guessed what it was as soon as she saw the label, saying:

"That's the gay guy's wine, the flavour is really complex, I drink it often."

Sure enough, she drank plenty and seemed relaxed. Over the course of the banquet somebody mentioned Peach and that person was promptly kicked under the table. Nobody expected Mali to remain calm, to take the initiative and ask:

"You heard that Peach got married to a millionaire? You heard he has several hundred million?"

Everybody guessed that Pang De had exaggerated to her. In any case, we all needed to protect Pang De's vanity and nobody recklessly corrected the figure. Jian Mali didn't investigate any further. Pang De's wine had a marvellous effect on her. She regularly recalled past events and didn't hold back in the least in revealing details about her life in New York. It was her initiative to bring up the affair on top of the tower at the Children's Palace. She said that the idea of jumping from that tower wasn't even all that scary.

"In Manhattan, I was on the verge of jumping from a thirty-seven-storey building! Much taller than the little tower at the Children's Palace.

When she said this, she looked at us honestly and said:

"It's not only because of love but because of rent, because, because... of heartbreak."

It was difficult for her to choose the word heartbreak, and a stream of tears suddenly welled up in her eyes.

"I had already written my suicide note, I was at the top of the building and you know who saved me?"

The air suddenly became tense, everybody looked at her intensely, guessing who she would name. I remember, at the time I was inclined to visualise, so in my head the image that leapt to mind was that of Madonna. I watched her lips, facing me. She distinctly but softly uttered Pang De's name. Jian Mali sipped a mouthful of wine and smiled a little.

"Excuse our carelessness or ignorance."

"Don't guess, you won't guess." She suddenly used her finger to point at her mixed-race girl. "It was Lucia. Lucia was just five that year. She chased me to the top of the building in her pyjamas. She said to me, 'Mummy, don't leave me. I'll jump with you. Carry me, we'll jump together'."

The table was silent for a while. Nobody dared to speak and everybody's gaze was focused on Lucia's face. Lucia was a beautiful girl with long legs, flaxen hair and azure-tinted eyes. We very rarely see blue eyes. It was difficult to determine Lucia's expression, it showed that she was innocent and precocious; shy yet fearless. She had been playing a video game with her younger brother the whole time but at that moment she lifted her head and looked at her mother reproachfully. She said in English:

"Mummy, you're drunk, I forbid you to say anything else."

Jian Mali stuck out her tongue but said no more. To ease the tension, somebody cautiously struck up a conversation with Lucia.

"Lucia, you little beauty, do you like Madonna?"

Lucia shook her head.

"Nah, Madonna's old news."

About the Author

Su Tong, pen name of Tong Zhonggui, was born in Suzhou, East China in 1963. He rose to international acclaim after his book *Wives and Concubines* was made into a blockbuster film *Raise the Red Lantern* by director Zhang Yimou, featuring actress Gong Li. The film won a BAFTA award in 1993 for best non-english language film. He was the joint winner of the prestigious Mao Dun Literature Prize for his novel *Yellow Bird* in 2015 (published in English as *Shadow of the Hunter* in 2020). His earlier novel *The Boat to Redemption* was awarded the Man Asia Literature Prize in 2009. Su Tong, currently resident in Nanjing, is a prolific, unconventional writer. Having grown up in the Cultural Revolution, his writing depicts everyday life in China with a dark twist. In addition to his many striking novels, he has also written hundreds of short stories.

About the Translator

Honey Watson is a science fiction writer and translator living in Las Vegas, Nevada. She is a translator of both fiction and non-fiction from Mandarin into English, holding degrees from University College London and Peking University, Beijing. Her debut novel, *Lessons in Birdwatching*, was released by Angry Robot books in August 2023.

ABOUT **SINO**IST BOOKS

We hope you enjoyed these Midnight Stories.

SINOIST BOOKS brings the best of Chinese fiction to English-speaking readers. We aim to create a greater understanding of Chinese culture and society, and provide an outlet for the ideas and creativity of the country's most talented authors.

To let us know what you thought of this book, or to learn more about the diverse range of exciting Chinese fiction in translation we publish, find us online. If you're as passionate about Chinese literature as we are, then we'd love to hear your thoughts!

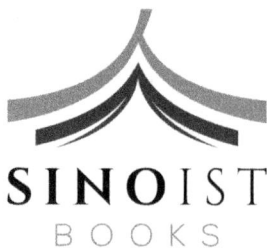

SINOIST
BOOKS

sinoistbooks.com • @sinoistbooks